THE UNUSUAL HISTORY OF MY WORLD

THE UNUSUAL HISTORY OF MY WORLD

AGAINST ALL OBSTACLES

David Singer

ISBN: 978-1722635046
LCCN: 2018908846
Imprint Name: Aventura, Florida. USA

Disclaimer
This story is based on some real events, however after multiple interviews
and research were attempted, I was unable confirm many of the events
that I describe. That is why I consider this to be a work of **fiction**. Names,
characters, businesses, places, events and incidents are either the products of my
imagination or used in a fictitious manner. Any resemblance to actual persons,
living or dead, or actual events is purely coincidental.

DEDICATION

This book is dedicated to my mother and father and to all those men and women who feel their life is detained whenever they face important obstacles. After you read this book you will feel that one never has to give up. Even when you face impossible obstacles you must look for alternative solutions. Here you will also see that life is good when you are happy, but life is even better when others are made happy because of your acts. Those were my parent's thoughts. I have tried to make these life principals mine also.

TABLE OF CONTENTS

PROLOGUE

My maternal grandmother Mary was born in Vienna, Austria. At a very young age her wealthy family moved to Poland, and very soon after, at the very young age of 17 she was married off to my grandfather Morris. He was an older and very well to do businessman in Warsaw. Once I was told that he had a tremendous reputation of warding off the continuous pursuit of dozens of Jewish fathers trying to marry their daughters to wealthy, educated, and very good looking Jewish men. The day he met my grandmother, who was a second cousin on his father's side, magic happened. He fell blindly in love with what he considered to be the most lovely and exquisite woman he had ever seen. He referred to her as "main meidele," "my dearest find," "The sunshine of my eyes." These are difficult phrases to translate, because all the conversations were in Yiddish. Almost all my family were multilingual, they spoke Russian, Romanian, German, and Hebrew. However, Yiddish was the everyday conversation language, especially when in the presence of family and friends.

Soon after they were married, they moved to Botosani, Romania, were my mother Theresa, was born. Later the family moved to Chernovitz, a city known for its culture and arts, this city at that time, was part of Romania. There he opened a clothing store that prospered immediately. It became a very well-known and established firm in the area. My grandfather, an extrovert by nature, traveled to Paris, France and brought only the best clothes that were available. He was also a fantastic salesman. He knew how to attract the wealthier portion of the population to his shop for special clothing for special events.

My father's family on the other hand were from a very small town called Viznitza. The town was mainly known because it was the home to a very famous rabbi, head of a Talmudic Yeshiva, The Viznitzer Rebbe, who was very well known all over Europe and in the Hasidic world. Students who emerged from that school were considered especially prepared in the ways of the Torah. My father never got to know his father. In those days, in the early 1900's, any infection, bad cold or whatever that befell the very poor, usually ended in death. Famines were common, and one took my grandfather's life at a very early stage. My paternal grandmother was a tough and determined lady cared for her five children with all her strength and ability. She had already lost two husbands to illness and my grandfather was the third. My father, whose name was Mendel, was a very bright fellow and helped his brothers and sisters gather sufficient food for everyday survival. He used to talk to me about how he survived his adolescent years. My grandmother learned how to assist the local bread bakery owner and was given whatever bread was not sold for her family. I remember that my father used to tell me that he used to take care of the horses owned by the carriage owners in the town. He also used to shovel snow and clean the street sidewalks for a few coins during winter. During summers he used to help the local cow owners milk their cows and deliver the full metal milk containers door to door to the well-to-do customers. My father also used to go to Jeider (Hebrew school) every day. He talked of being so tired by the time he finished his chores that when he would get back to the single room they all shared, he would fall asleep without eating, even times when there was something to eat. The winters were harsh. He mentioned one particular winter that he could not forget, he repeatedly mentioned it, when they did not have sufficient money to buy oil for a heating furnace contraption that they had in the room. They almost froze to death. All six of them would curl up and hug each other to create warmth between them. "That's the way it was on those horribly cold Romanian winters," he would always say remembering.

The years passed, my father received a good Judaic education and was very well educated in mathematics as well. He had learned life's realities at a very early age. This prepared him for the future challenges in his life. Before the age of 17 he left Viznitza and went to the nearest commercial city, Chernovitz. He managed to get temporary jobs in several town stores. The fact that he was very handy, very handsome, had beautiful handwriting plus the fact that he was willing to do whatever he was asked, got him through the first few years. He was a fast learner and all his employers hated to see him leave whenever he found a better paying job. After he was 24 years old he was caught by the Romanian army and drafted. He was forced to work as a bomb shelter digger. All the Jews in his Romanian army group worked digging ditches, in preparation for the defense of their country from the advancing German army. They were sure the Germans would take over the country. He spoke to me of very hard years and of harsh treatment in the army. When I asked him if all the soldiers were treated badly. He responded, "Yes, but we the Jewish ones were always given the hardest and most dangerous tasks." There was no secret about the extreme anti-Semitism that existed in most of Europe, and Romania was no exception.

After my father's three-year stint in the army was over, he returned to Chernovitz. World War II had begun, and everyone was in an extreme state of nervousness. It was very difficult to find a job. Due to his hardship in the army, he had lost weight and his usual handsome demeanor had visibly suffered. He was lucky to be recognized by a former employer who gave him a letter of recommendation and directed him to my grandfather Morris store. There he was immediately hired. initially he was told that he would work only for food and board. Business in my grandfather's store had gone down because of the war. There were not many social events to dress for. Everyone's main question was, "Would the Germans invade Romania?" Many people had started to make a plan B. "How to get out of Romania? Where to go?" Everyone attempted to sell their properties and belongings to leave with some money. They needed some economic security in-order to re-establish themselves somewhere far from the war. The money itself was worth less and less each day. Devaluation was the name of the game. The natural thing to do was to attempt to convert or sell their holdings and accept only gold or other valuable jewelry as payment. This was with the hope that these precious items would maintain their value in other countries where there was no war.

My father adapted immediately to my grandfather's ways and in no time won over the appreciation of all the members of his boss' family. He had made himself indispensable to my grandfather. Due to grandfather Morris' continuous trips, he was placed in charge of the family business. My father's very outgoing personality was easy prey for my mother who looked for any excuse to come to the shop every day, with the difficult to hide motive, to see and to talk to my father. The romance developed openly and, although my grandfather had planned to marry her off to a wealthy and well-educated man, he readily accepted my father, who had shown his ability to accommodate and resolve all the problems that arose in these very difficult times. They were married in an intimate ceremony in 1937. For the next few years my parents lived in constant fear of the rumors of the approaching German Hitlerian army. Rumors of all kinds and types arose every moment. Information that they received was mostly brought from those that dared to travel toward the northern frontiers of Romania. There were constant movements of soldiers. Everyone felt that what was happening was like an unreal nightmare story. Little by little the food shortage became worse, and the mass migration of people started. When they consulted the leaving neighbors most of them were in terror and didn't know where to head or what to do. The confusion was total. My mother, an extremely beautiful woman, had been advised not to leave the house they lived in. To be out in the streets was dangerous. Many cases of rape had been reported in many of the occupied cities of the north. Then one grey and stormy day the German Army arrived in Bucharest. A strict curfew was imposed. My father had already been meeting secretly with a recently formed underground movement. This movement was made up of many ex-soldiers both Jewish and non-Jewish, whose objective was to destroy or impede the advancement of the Germans in Romania. They had been able to find rifles and other war implements abandoned by what was left of the retreating Romanian Army. It was a sad moment for my parents. It was a sad moment for everyone. My father joined the clandestine movement and left the city. My parents did not know if they would ever meet again. My maternal grandparents had left in one of the last trains to head towards Italy. They went with their youngest daughter and no luggage. My mother refused to travel with them for fear of losing contact with my father when, and if, he were to return. She stayed behind with her very loyal Rajila, a Romanian employee that had taken care of my mother since her birth.

Three weeks later, the Germans began to make a census of the Jewish population. The German commander wanted to know the exact address of all the Jews in Chernovitz. The German SS were charged with gathering that information. They promised many Romanian non-Jews they would receive special favors if they helped supply the names and addresses of the local Jews. My parents later told me that the Germans were successful in getting all the information they needed. All the men in the Jewish neighborhoods were arrested a few days later. Most prisoners were told they would be taken to forced-work camps. The women, children and very old men were separated and then placed on a train, huddled into cramped wagons with standing room only space. Their destination was not known. No one dared ask questions, they all knew what the consequences were. A blunt rifle's impact on the head was the usual result for those that dared ask. The resulting wound usually became infected and they would shoot to kill those that got sick and could not work. Some were known to be deported and ended up in the gas camps of Auschwitz. My mother ended up in one of those trains. My mother told me her story, "I was crying like most of the women, many so old and sick that they could hardly walk. They were forced to crawl into the wagons. "The German soldiers and their Romanian collaborators showed no mercy, no pity." My mother described them as "heartless inhumane devils." After a few days of travel and multiple stops, they were permitted to disembark to relieve themselves. Unfortunately, the stench from the windowless wagons was unbearable. Over 70 hours had elapsed since they left Chernovitz. They were all on their feet in the wagons. There was standing room only. It would have been impossible to sit or lie down without crushing one another. No food or water had been permitted to be taken aboard or anything at all. Everyone that had boarded the train was not permitted to take anything with them. My mother had tried to describe the horror that she had gone through in those many hours that seemed eternal. "The constant crying and moaning of the children, the elderly and those that were very ill made things unbearable." When the German guards finally opened the doors to her wagon, there were over a dozen people that had died, many due to suffocation, or a heart attacks, who knows why or how? The next thing they knew was that they were herded into uncovered army trucks. The bitter cold of January made their life even more miserable. The trucks stopped close to a semi frozen creek, and they were permitted to drink the water and wash their hands and faces. The soldiers continued with their brutal and inhuman behavior. One soldier shot an old man that resisted an effort to force him to walk faster. His accompanying family didn't even dare complain or try to help him. The moment was full of hate and hopelessness. After several hours, the trucks arrived into a makeshift camp full of bungalow-like buildings. My mother was led to cabin #76 with 18 other women and seven very old men. The women with children were not taken off the trucks, and they were never heard from again. There were rumors that the children were separated from their mothers and either sent for adoption to German homes or killed. Their well-known objective was to make the Jewish race disappear. This statement was often heard among the German soldiers.

On day two, they were finally permitted access to the garbage remains of the Germans officers' kitchen. The garbage cans were principally full of potato skins that had recently been disposed of. They were given the tools necessary to make a fire and were given a water filled pot to cook the potato peels. That was to be their principal food for the next several weeks. They had no clothes to change to. Their clothes were fetid and torn and worn. They had no alternative, and continuously worried about their fate. They asked themselves, "What are they going to do to us next?" They never knew what to expect. No one spoke to them and they were not in contact with any of the other bungalows. The guards changed frequently and although some of the younger women attempted to form some type of camaraderie with them, it was useless as new guard appeared on the next shift. The Germans were careful not to be distracted from their work.

After a few weeks of the same daily schedule, all they could think about was the warm potato skin soup they were going to make themselves. Everyone had lost weight and looked horrendous. My mother had no idea what she looked like, there was no mirror or anything in which to see a reflection of herself. Then on a sunny day, they realized they had lost track of what day it was. There was one very orthodox old man in her group that kept on scribbling a number on the wall for each new day, but every time it rained his numbers vanished from the wall because there were water leaks everywhere. He wanted to keep a track of Shabbat. Suddenly, one day they let them out of the bungalows and gave them a stripped jail style uniform, with a Jewish star symbol attached to their left side. They asked them to take off their clothes and throw them in a furnace that they had a lit for that purpose. There was no such thing as being ashamed of one's nakedness. The term shame had been lost with all the suffering. Who could think of sexuality after these horrendous moments. The very smelly bungalows and very ill and dying roommates predominated their thoughts. They were ushered into a shower water stall and permitted to shower in the cold of the winter. Then they had to wait until the sun and cold wind helped them dry up. They were then ordered to clean up the bungalow with what-ever they could find, which was not much. After the ordeal was over they all felt better and were treated to a hard loaf of bread. This was the first solid food, a piece of hard bread, they had since their arrival to this detention camp.

The following week, almost everyone in their small bun-galow-like-quarters fell sick. Five days later two elderly men passed away after horrible nights and days with high fever, their coughing seemingly unstoppable. The fear of infection permeated the bungalow. My mother assumed that they had died of pneumonia. My mother was one of the lucky few that did not contract the horrible illness, she attributed the sick-ness to the shower on that horrid cold day. They all assumed that this horrible ordeal, their collective illness, was caused by the extreme low temperatures and their nakedness.

Unknown to my mother at first, one of the German soldiers kept his eyes glued on her and became very aware of her beauty. After seeing her nakedness as she showered he called several of his comrades to see the beautiful body. One of her bunkmates Marcella, alerted my mother of the impending possibility that she was going to be selected by the Germans for 'you know what.' She warned her to be careful. That is when my mother realized that everyone had seen her nakedness and that she might have attracted the soldiers that were on guard at that moment. That night she didn't sleep out of fear. This continued for many days. One day after two dead bodies were removed from their cabin, a German officer came into the compound and selected my mother for work at the officer's food preparation center. She was in tears at first, because she expected to be raped or taken advantage of. To her surprise the person in charge was very friendly and told her not to fear that nothing would happen to her. However, she was very scared, she didn't know what to expect. My mother was taken to a bathroom and told to bathe. She was then given a waitress uniform. Then one of the guards gave her lipstick and creams and told her to use them on her. She was going to be a waitress for the camp's officer's food preparation center. My mother mind was very confused, she was fearful of what this was leading to. My mother had no choice but to obey the instructions she was given. That day was the first day that she ate a decent meal since her ordeal began. She was now in the hands of a Romanian cook, who instructed her on how to serve the military officers correctly and warned her to be very careful.

"If they talk to you just nod with your head. Do not look at them straight into their eyes. Obey everything they tell you, don't hesitate. They selected you to work here in the dining room, you are very lucky. If they like you, they won't send you to the gas chambers." She then asked him, how he knew that that was their destiny. He told her that he understood German and that he overheard everything they talked about. The cook told my mother that he was fearful for his life also. He told her that the Germans had not discovered that his grandmother was Jewish. He said, "The day they discover that, I will also be going to the death camp. I had my own restaurant in Bistrita, a small city in Romania, and they arrested all my employees because they were Jewish and as punishment for catering to Jews they sent me to cook in this camp. I was lucky that my wife and children were visiting with their aunt on the island of Crete in Greece. You see my wife is also Jewish, and so are my children. I insisted they leave three months ago." He continued to tell my mother that he arrived three weeks ago, and they treated him like a slave. "They do not get frequent deliveries of food from Germany, so I have to ration the officers' portions which is something they complain about and threaten to send me to the Jewish barracks, or bungalows as they call them." All the events that follow are a recompilation of my recollection from what both my parents related to me in different stages of my adult life. "She had no choice," was something she reiterated many times.

CHAPTER 1

MY MOTHER THE WAITRESS

The first time she came into the dining-hall, there were a dozen German officers. Two of them wore SS insignia on their right arm. The one at the head of the table, an older German, seemed to be in charge. One of the officers with the SS label whistled at her and commented to the rest, "What a nice pair of breasts this Jewish broad has." Another one mentioned something about her "nice behind." She tried to ignore the remarks. They did not know that she understood some German because of her fluent Yiddish. The commanding officer showed his distaste at their remarks and insinuated, in a grumbling manner, "Do not be distracted with our detained servers, we have more important things to think about." The SS officer in a probable attempt to pull rank, got up and showed the commanding officer the middle finger. This act was not tolerated by the officers loyal to their commander. They got up and asked the SS officer to either respect the commander or leave the room. The offending SS officer got up and left without finishing his served meal. The other SS officers followed him out. My mother tried her best to ignore the stressful events. She attempted to go back to the kitchen, when one of the officers, stopped her telling her not to leave yet. "Bring us some coffee," he said. When she returned, she caught the Germans in a heated argument. They were talking about the SS officers lack of respect and the fact that they had to obey the base commander whether they agreed with him or not. When my mother started to clean up the tables, all the German officers had left. The SS German that had caused the altercation came back in to the dining room asking her to serve him his meal again, he spoke in broken Romanian. She answered that she did not think there was anything left. She summoned the cook and he offered to cook some eggs for him. He refused and roughly grabbed my mother and started to hug her and feel her body. The cook immediately left, and she was alone with her intruder. He evidently had intentions of violating her, when suddenly the commanding officer with two of his men entered the dining room again. My mother imagined that the cook had informed them of what was happening. One of the officers grabbed the SS officer and gave him a blow to his chin. The SS officer got up from floor and before he could take out his pistol, he was overpowered and handcuffed. My mom was excused and taken back to her bungalow in that very cold and snowy night. Her roommates were glad to see her, they thought that she had been another victim of the Nazis. They saw the tears in her face and her torn blouse and decided to leave her alone and not ask the obvious questions they had. My mother started praying silently, all the prayers that she had learned by heart from school and from her religious father. She had been feeling terrible, and now this new incident made her think again, that her days were numbered. She told me that at this point she dreamt of my father and had illusions of him coming in with his underground troops and rescuing her. She said "the Shema" several times.

The next day, she was again picked up by a different guard and taken to the officers' kitchen. The Romanian cook was fearful that the SS guy would take revenge. She was given a new, less revealing blouse to put on, as part of her waitress uniform. She then proceeded to serve breakfast without incident. The SS men were absent. During breakfast a communication officer came in and gave the commander a note. The commander got up and announced that he had just been relieved of his duties and was being sent to a new command post in Poland. He informed the officers that the new commander would be arriving in the next train that afternoon. He saluted his officers and wished them luck, then he made the Sig Heil salute and left. That evening a complete new set of officers came to the dining room. There were also several new SS officers present. The cook, who was my mom's new ally, said that another cook, the one working in the soldiers' dining facilities, had told him that the SS arrested the officer, was the one that caused this sudden change of commander.

The new commanding officer was a man in his early sixties and had a very gentle voice, he seemed to be new in this type of commanding position. He began to talk introducing himself to the officers present, and seemed to be very kind, very different from the one my mother had met the day before. He called my mother over and asked her for her name. She told him, "Theresa," and he told her that "From now on, I will call you Terry." The new SS officers were very respectful, and did not participate in the war discussions, they kept to themselves. However, they did take notes all the time. They were very young, and their inexperience was noticeable. My mother asked the cook if there were any leftovers to take back with her to her bunk. He told her that he was afraid of being caught. She did manage to get some leftovers and wrap them in a newspaper. Thus, she was able to get away with some cooked potatoes, and shreds of stew hidden under her coat without his knowledge. As soon as she got back, she distributed everything to the very old and fragile roommates. She was approached by all in her bungalow and gave them a rundown of her last two days experience.

In the middle of that same night, my mother was woken up and told to put on her coat and follow a guard. Everyone who was asleep woke up and attempted to protest her removal from the bungalow. They were warned to abstain, and not get involved or they would sleep outside, where it had not stopped snowing. She was taken to a large building that she later found out, was the commanders headquarters. This was the building where the camps commanders sleeping quarters were. She was left in a fancy living room area with a gigantic bookcase full of German books. She saw Renaissance art in picture frames which she recognized from her studies. My mother had no idea where the camp was. She didn't know if she was in Austria, Romania or Germany. After a long wait, the new commanding officer walked in. Fully dressed, with several rows of shiny metal medals and other decorations. He sat down in front of her and with a very soft and endearing voice said. "I'm sorry to have brought you here at this hour. I hope you can forgive me. I want you to know that I had you come here for your own good. That SS officer that attempted to seduce you, has important connections in Berlin and had the last commander transferred. That SS officer is still here, and we think that he will attempt to harm you. I want to make you an offer, you can think about it, you can decide whenever you want. I recommend you do it soon. How good is your German?" She answered with the truth, that she spoke Yiddish and that it was very similar to German. She told him she could understand if it were spoken slowly. "Ok Terry, I want you to live in my apartment. This way you will keep me company and you will be safe. You will have food and clothing and I will guarantee you that by doing this you will survive. If you decide not to accept, I cannot guarantee what will happen to you and to the others in this camp. It's really not in my hands. The SS is very strong and their leader in Berlin has our Chief commander's ears. But, if you are with me you are safe." My mother, with fear in her eyes started to uncontrollably accumulate tears, and she did not answer. "Dear Terry, he said, I know what is going through your mind. I am a good person, I will not harm you. I have a daughter your age. I will respect you. No one has to know what we do or what we don't do in our privacy." Theresa thought of the alternatives she had. The Commander had introduced himself as Hans. Hans left her alone in the room, to give her time to digest his proposal.

My mother reminded herself that she had been married for seven years now and had not become pregnant. She wondered what would happen if she accepted this German's offer and became pregnant with his child? She thought that she would definitely kill herself if that happened. It must have been almost five in the morning when Hans came back into the living room and asked her if she wanted to be taken back to her bungalow. My mother knew that either she accepted his survival offer or faced the alternative, which would be a sure rape and probably death.

My mother told me that she followed Hans into his sleeping quarters and laid down in his bed and fell asleep, almost instantly. The next morning, she woke up around midday. She was alone in the room. Hans had left her a note. "Sleep, and rest, you are not a waitress anymore, you are my protégé." Theresa showered and found clothes Hans had left on a table to change in to. At approximately one pm, Hans came in with food and a bottle of wine. He showed it to Theresa and told her that he had gotten this wine in a Jewish shop in Berlin, and that it was kosher. She told him that she doesn't drink alcohol, but he insisted she try. It will make everything easier, he said.

Hans started to tell my mother about his life. "I was born in Munich and became an architect. I married my university sweetheart and had one daughter. My wife died at an early age in a train crash and I brought up my daughter by myself. She now lives in Australia and has two children of her own. I was forced into accepting the army as my only professional choice due to the harsh economic reality that led to this horrible war. Since I had a reputation as a person that got things done effectively, I rose to the present status of commanding officer of this unit of prisoners of war camp, or detention camp, as it is officially called. I definitely have nothing against the Jews, in fact one of my university classmates in Berlin and several in my Post Graduate studies in Frankfurt were Jewish. I ate and made Shabbat with them on numerous occasions. I want you to know that the majority of Germans are not anti-Semites. However, our present leaders do not fall into that category."

CHAPTER 2

THE 'PROTÉGÉ'

Several weeks went by, my mother started to notice several things. First, that she had not gotten her menstrual period for over two months, which was about the time that she was detained by the Germans. Secondly, she had an urge to urinate with frequency, something unusual for her, and third her breasts had started to swell. She became worried, and constantly looked at her belly to see if that had changed in dimensions. The truth of the matter she said, is that in the last few weeks she had eaten much more than normal. Hans had permitted her to secretly take food to her friends at the bungalow. She also precured some old clothing for them. She attempted to explain her predicament. She explained that the commander had not touched her. Yes, she slept in his bed, but he has not touched her or seen her naked. She told me, "When I use the bathroom, he is not present." She thought that they definitely didn't believe a word she said. One day when she went to bring them some sweets that Hans had brought her, Marcella, her closest friend in the bungalow told her that she suspected that my mother was pregnant. They went to a corner of the bunk and she lifted up her dress, and upon observation, said that she definitely thought that I was pregnant. She reminded my mother that she had some mid-wife experience and that she knew how pregnant women look like and how they act. "Be careful, if they discover you are pregnant the Germans will get rid of you. They do not allow pregnant and especially Jewish women to give birth to live babies, or so we were told."

The news Marcella gave her, left her in deep thought. She remembered the night that my father Meyer, left for the underground movement, they had made intense love. That was over three months ago. Then my mother thought of the times she overslept in Hans' bed. "Had he slipped a sleeping pill into her regular tea before going to sleep? Did he have sex with me while I was asleep?" She told me that although she thought that to be highly unlikely, because she thought that a woman knows when someone has had sex with her, even when she is asleep. Hans treated her like if she was his daughter she insisted. "At no time did he even insinuate or attempt to befriend her in any manner that she would even remotely suspect of different intentions. In fact, the first few nights when she laid close to him, he would place an extra cover on her on very cold nights, and he always kept his distance. My mother had acquired a strange kind of confidence in this man.

Several weeks passed, and her belly was now noticeably bigger, her breasts were sensitive and became more swollen as the days passed. She then decided to tell Hans what she suspected. When she finally got the guts to speak about that possibility. His reaction was one of joy combined with one of fear. He told her, "I have never told anyone what I am about to tell you, I was also in the train accident that killed my wife and twenty other passengers. I was injured in the groin area and was told that I would never be able to have an erection because the nerves in that area were damaged beyond repair. I have become a sort of eunuch, in the biblical sense. We will have to tell everyone in the officer's quarters that the baby is mine, he said. If anyone finds out that you are pregnant from before, not even the fact that you are my protégé will save you. They will make you abort the baby and maybe even send you to one of those camps in Poland. She could not believe all that Hans had confided to her. The way he talked to her made her feel his sincerity, she felt that it was totally true. My mother knew she was a very attractive woman and had all the characteristics that any man would like to observe in a lady. She was tall, busty, and had a special glamour attached to her beautiful face and figure.

Hans had Theresa accompany him to the officers dining room and announced to all the officers with pride, that he was going to have a baby with Terry. Everyone applauded, even the three SS officers present. They congratulated Hans, some knew of his accident, but no one knew of its consequences. My mother was so grateful to Hans, that night she kissed and hugged him in gratitude for him being human, a gentleman, and for saving her and her baby.

CHAPTER 3

MY FATHER THE WAR HERO

My father, Mendel, had met regularly with a group of young ex-army friends. They discussed the unstoppable advancement of the German troops and the destruction they caused of everything that was in their way. Some of these men were Jewish but the majority were loyal Romanian Christians that wanted to do something for their country. They did not want to just sit around and wait to be imprisoned and be placed in obligated work force details by the invading army. These men were full of determination and hoped to carry out specific plans to deteriorate the German movement of troops, ammunition and food supply. They had found abandoned equipment that the Romanian army left after they disbanded and hid everything they could from sight. They knew that what they had planned to do was extremely risky and could easily mean a death squad if caught.

When they were informed that the Germans would be in their part of Romania in less than two weeks they decided to get together in a nearby abandoned train station and plan their strategy. All their relatives were informed and were told to tell anyone who asked, that they had left Romania for good, so that their absence would not arise when the Germans made their home inquiry. As they all knew the Germans had infiltrated the ranks of the government in many cities and had elaborated lists of Jewish homes as the enemies of "their glorious German army."

Their first mission was to destroy the rail tracks in several points in the direction to and from Germany. My father and a group of four men carried out a successful dynamite explosion. This first attempt went without incident and was done in the middle of the night to ensure no patrols were in the vicinity. Their second mission was to get to a nearby major German outpost and destroy a building where they suspected housed an important storage camp for their ammunition and gasoline supplies. They did not have reliable information. The Romanians that lived in that area were very scared and did not want to get involved with the underground groups. They knew that retaliation would occur, and that they would be the closest to the attacked site and most likely victims. There was one young woman, Ronnie, who was also an anti-German volunteer, she was the exception. Ronnie defied fear and accepted a role in this very dangerous mission. Their plan was that she would attempt to infiltrate the outpost as a saleswoman. Since she was, young and pretty they would probably let her in with a bicycle to sell cheese and with luck, without checking her background. The bike's back stool was full of Romanian white cheese. The day to attempt the incursion came. She was guided by a guard to the person in charge of buying produce and received payment immediately. She tried to make friendly gestures to the very young German guards who admired her physique and finally one of them broke protocol and came up to her and handed her a note and tried to be discreet. The note was in Romanian. It said, "meet you at the gate at eight tonight." She took a look and winked a positive response. That was her main purpose, to establish contact with someone inside.

That night Ronnie received instructions, to try to cultivate a friendship with that guard. They told her, "If necessary, promise him that you feel like getting involved sexually with him, but you need to get to know him better." She was a smart and a daring woman and knew what she had to do. That evening at the accorded time the guard appeared outside of the camp's gate and walked toward her. He immediately hugged her and wanted to involve her in a quickie. She evidently told him, "One second, not so fast. What do you think I am a prostitute? You do not even know me. What is your name?" He became disillusioned and wanted to leave and go back to the camp. He evidently was not allowed to leave the German outpost. She stopped him and insinuated that she knew of a place they could go and talk and get to know each other better. He hesitated but Ronnie had dressed in a manner so that any man would be attracted. She had a low cut, reveling blouse and short skirt. He readily accepted, and told her that he only had a few minutes, because if he was discovered, he would get into a lot of trouble. She took him to a nearby abandoned shack. She let him kiss her and then she told him that she had her menstrual period and could not do anything else. She told him that she would be going back to the outpost because she works for a cheese store and will need to deliver cheese again. She asked him if they could meet in the closed building in the camp. He told her that that place was off limits for him. Then on second thought he said that the guard assigned to that building was his best friend and he was sure he would let them in for a few minutes. She kissed him again and he left in a hurry. The plan to obtain information on that outpost before attempting this mission was initiated. My father was also involved in this mission, he was in the rescue detail in case Ronnie got detained or got into trouble. Meanwhile, his group received a message from another member of the underground informing them that an underwater demolition man was urgently needed in Constanta a Romanian port in the Black sea. My father happened to know someone in Chernovitz that was an expert swimmer who had trained for the Olympics. He thought that this friend, could do this type of a job. The question was how to find him in the war-torn city? Should he risk his life was his constant question.

A few days later Ronnie went back to the camp with her full cheese basket. Underneath the basket the group explosive expert had placed four dynamite sticks with an igniting mechanism. Ronnie had her instructions. She was to place the dynamite in the angle closest to the only window in the building which looked to the outside of the camp. She should not attempt to do anything else herself, other than place the dynamite sticks in that place. My father had told her "Abort the mission if things become complicated." Ronnie was again permitted to enter with no special ID check. They remembered her from the first time. In the camp, by the entrance door was her friend the guard, he had been desperately waiting for her to appear again, and here she was. He himself accompanied her to the produce delivery kitchen area. Once she was paid she told him she was in a hurry to leave the camp, she had another delivery, she said. The guard reminded her of their deal. She winked at him and they proceeded to the building. He told her that he had tried to find a better place but that was the only one were they could have privacy. He reminded her that no one was allowed in there. She asked why? He mentioned something about the fact that it was full of armament, and gasoline for the convoys that came from Germany. He told her that this was the main refueling station in the area. When the guard's friend at the main building door saw them coming he hesitated, and a discussion began. After 20 minutes of arguing. Ronnie was ready to abort the idea of continuing, when her guard friend came up to her and told her, "Look I have a problem. He won't let me in to this restricted building unless I make you promise him that once I am finished with you, you give him a chance also. He hasn't been with a woman since he left Stuttgart, over a year ago." Ronnie showed her angry face at the insinuation and said she would do no such thing. "What do you think I am a whore." He begged her and then said." Look, I'll promise him but the only reason I am going in there with you is because you are very handsome, he is not my type and I am not a whore." However, Ronnie went up to his friend and whispered in his ear, "see you soon" and Ronnie went in through a side door, with her bicycle. The guard reiterated that she should not touch anything, that this place is off limits. "Find a comfortable place where we can be together and come back to the door, so I will come in first, and then my friend." Ronnie saw exactly what she needed, she took the bag with the dynamite rolls, and hid them right by the window facing the outside of the camp. It was the ideal place they had instructed her. Then she purposely cut her lip and came out of the door to the expecting guards. They looked at her with horror as they saw her bloodied face. She simulated crying, said she fell and hurt herself and asked to go to a bathroom to clean up her face. The guards became worried that someone might see her and asked her to leave and come back another day. The mission was almost accomplished. Late that night one of the men in my father's group who was an experienced mountain climber went up to the indicated window and cut a hole with a glass cutter and gently lowered a gasoline-soaked sheet unto the direction that Ronnie had indicated.

He then lit a match and jumped to the ground then ran safely to his waiting group. The explosion was immediate, and the resulting fire could be seen for miles away. They left that same night to Constanta in an old jeep they had inherited from the Romanian army. My father returned to Chernovitz to look for his friend the Olympic swimmer.

CHAPTER 4

MY FATHER'S SEARCH

My father told me that he arrived to Chernovitz, very early in the morning, dressed as a farmer. He had put on a white wig that he had found in an abandoned store. He did not have ID papers and was afraid of being detained. He figured they would not bother with an older looking man. The first thing he did was go by the house in search for my mother. The house was abandoned, and he spoke to someone he recognized from the neighborhood. She told him that Rajila, his wife's nanny was in a house in Hernstrasse, near his fathers-in-law closed store. He assumed that she was staying in the house of one of my grandfather's employees. He found her there and she was so glad to see him. She told him the whole story, how the Germans came and simply arrested all the Jews in the area. They didn't touch Rajila because she was Christian and was not on the list that some neighbor had given the SS officers. She had heard that they put her on a train going north but had no idea what was true and what was a rumor. Rajila also told him that she had a package that my mother had left her in case my father returned. Rajila said she wasn't sure of anything anymore. Rumors came and went. Rajila proceeded to search for the package and returned with it. My father opened it up and it was a package full of gold coins that my grandfather had left my mother, in case she decided to attempt to leave Romania. He took some of the coins and returned the rest to the package. My father gave several of the gold coins to Rajila in case she needed them. She replied that "Your Theresa left me sufficient for a lifetime." My father left in search of that friend, "The Swimmer," and was told that he had moved to Bucharest, Romania's capital. My father searched for anyone who could inform him where my mother had been taken to, but he could not find any of his Jewish acquaintances. The synagogues were all abandoned, the Germans had made sure of that. He then went back to Rajila's house and asked her to let him stay there for a day or two. She, of course, was delighted. The next morning, he sent her out to investigate where my mother could be held. She went to all the still opened government offices without success. Then she happened to see the woman that had once been in charge of my grandfather's properties in Chernovitz. She recognized and greeted her. This lady was one that really loved my grandparents. She told Rajila that she knew someone in the new Romanian Government who was in friendly terms with the new German Commander. She would try to find out if they had any information. Three days went by with no news, my father could not wait any longer, so he left for Bucharest on a train, not without the continuous fear of being detained at any moment. Once in Bucharest he went straight to The Gymnasium a well-known swimming school that everyone knew had a professional swimming pool and inquired about his friend. He was very lucky, they knew of his whereabouts and gave him his temporary address. My father went to the address, but it was door to door with the local Gestapo headquarters. It was swarming with SS officers. He waited in a nearby café, until nightfall and then he dared go into the building. His friend was there, living in the basement, employed as a cleaning helper. He welcomed my father and after hearing my father's objective in searching for him, he remained reluctant to participate in such a daring adventure. Still, my father's very persuasive arguments finally changed his mind. He had recently lost his wife to an unknown illness and was quite depressed. The next morning, they both returned to Chernovitz, this time in a small urban decrepit bus that had to be pushed several times to re-start the failing motor. When they made a stop in Rajila's place she had information that might be useful. According to one source, my mother was in a camp in Germany. According to another source she was in Cluj-Napocain, Romania, a town that had a big Nazi army regiment. That town according to the Swimmer was an extreamely dangerous place to visit, especially for a Jew.

My father knew that there was an important mission waiting for "The Swimmer" and he had to get him to Constanta.

CHAPTER 5

CONSTANTA ON THE BLACK SEA

onstanta is a city on the shores of the Black Sea, in south-
ern Romania. Its history goes back over 2000 years. It is
the Home of the Romanian navy. My father had agreed to
meet his group, close to a museum near the Navy yards. Meyer
was almost a week behind his group, but he thought he had the
man capable of doing that very special underwater job. The
swimmer had no experience diving, he was an Olympic swimming champion. However, they had no one else who had the
experience of swimming and of putting on the rubber swimming garments that he was used to wearing when practicing
for the Olympics and especially in the middle of the winter.
They were able to find diving equipment and also found an
older man who was willing to instruct the swimmer in the art
of diving with oxygen tanks attached to his back. This old
timer gave them the equipment that he had used in the past.

The great problem was obtaining oxygen tanks that were useable and functionable. Their group leader, a man in his forties, had the plan. A German submarine was docked in the port and they had found out that it was to leave for a destination to the Caribbean Sea. That's what informants had heard on a shortwave radio. The instructions were to disable the ship and any German ship in the harbor. They had sufficient dynamite, but none of them had the expertise on how to handle these explosives underwater. Again, they called on Ronnie to see if she could infiltrate the German area. She dressed again in a very provocative manner and went to a coffee shop right near the navy base the Germans had occupied. It didn't take long for the sailors to start making remarks as to her beauty and several attempted to offer her a beer. It was not until one with an officer uniform came up to her with a bottle of beer that she accepted. He went straight to the point. Are you Romanian? What are you doing later tonight? I am off duty at eight pm. While he attempted to get a response out of her, another German officer with an apparent higher rank, his hat with several stars, approached her and sat right next to her on the opposite site of the first officer. The first officer gave him the hail Hitler salute and left the table. This one was the gentlemanly type and ordered a soup for both of them. While this was going on the bar owner or someone that looked like he was in charge, observed what was happening. When Ronnie happened to look in his direction, he motioned to her with a side movement of his head to leave or to move away. Ronnie did not understand what was happening, so she played it safe and told the German that she needed to go to the bathroom. Her German was understandable, and the new German officer nodded in agreement, and told her to hurry back. When Ronnie approached the man behind the counter to ask directions to the bathroom. He told her get out of here, there is going to be an explosion in here in a few minutes. He followed her to the back and so did the three other employees. They started to run for their lives when suddenly a big explosion rocked the bar. A blaze ensued. There must have been 25 Germans there and not one was able to get out alive. Ronnie was taken to a safe house and this is how they met Michelle, a Frenchman, who had formed a local resistance group. Ronnie was related to him, she thanked him for saving her life and eventually told him of her intentions and what she really was doing for the group. She took him to my father's group, where they joined forces. One of Michelle's men had been in the Romanian navy and was trained with underwater explosives. Their luck was absolute, three hours later the group managed to place three explosive charges on the submarine and two nearby German cargo ships right next to each other in the same harbor quarter. Everything worked out perfectly because the commotion that the bar explosion made followed a complete mobilization of the SS guards and the rest of the occupying army and they concentrated on trying to search and apprehend the culprits. Never did they suspect that their submarine and the other German navy ships were the real and main target. So, the security at the harbor were totally lax. The complete group got on a small towing boat and made their way to a 20-mile location in total darkness. They feared complete mobilization after this very effective attempt to disrupt their occupying efforts.

My father's group had grown to more than 18 men and the one woman, Ronnie. They decided to leave this area and were directed to Sibiu, a city in Transylvania in central Romania. This City was known for its Germanic architecture, as it was part of an area that housed many Saxon settlers in the 12th Century. There were many remains of medieval walls and towers. They had decided to go there because Michelle had been told that the city was under complete German control and that most of the Romanian resistance were in jeopardy of either being killed or sent to the Polish extermination camps. These brave men had put up incredible resistance but were outgunned and totally outnumbered by the advancing German tank division. The trip there was going to be long and very dangerous. They had to separate into groups of six, so they would not be so visible to the many guard positions all along their objective. My father's group avoided the roads and traveled throughout the night. They almost always found a friendly place to sleep over and were always offered whatever food was available by the rural farmers and countrymen. One night, they were near a well-lit farm and as they were approaching two big Doberman started to pursue the group. They had discussed that something like that could happen. Many of the farmers had watch dogs. Bands of Gypsies were known to invade and steal from these rural outposts. The farmers had little or no way of defending themselves, so they employed dogs to try to scare them off. My father was jumped by one and after attempting to control him was bitten on his right foot by the dog. That bite later became infected and was one of the reasons why my father had to separate temporarily from the group. He did not want to slow them down and slow down their immediate objectives.

After the dog incident, the farm owner was very helpful and let my father stay there for several weeks. A nearby doctor visited him and aided in the curing of his wound. That dog became my father's friend and protector. He must have realized that he had bitten the wrong person. My father's kindness won him over. At one point my father seriously thought of accepting the dog, as the owner offered him as protection on his continuous travels. My father thanked him for his generosity and told him that it would slow him down when he attempted to get rides on the roads. No one was going to accept him with a dog, and especially a Doberman. He arrived in Sibiu and it took him several days to find his group. Two of the men had been arrested in a roadblock. They had no Identification on them and were detained for questioning and investigation. Michelle the Frenchmen had been able to communicate with his family in Lyon, France, and had to rush back to help with his ailing mother. They had made several plans to place explosives in an area where they parked over 30 tanks but did not have sufficient explosives to do an efficient job. My father's group decided to see if they could reach a local resistance group. They needed help. My father had gold coins and was able to find a safe shelter and food for his group.

CHAPTER 6

MY MOTHER'S PREGNANCY

As the weeks turned into months, my mother's belly became very noticeable and she had many bouts of nausea, vomiting and ill feeling during many of the advancing gestation stages. The camp's German general physician cared for her and was her frequent companion. He turned out to have a Jewish mother which he hid from everyone because of the implication. One who is born in a Jewish womb is Jewish, according to the Jewish religion. Although his father tried to hide that fact, his mother continually reminded him of his maternal heritage. He also confided to her that he definitely felt that he was gay. He was very ashamed of this fact because it was considered a crime and he knew that if found out he would lose his medical license and be banished from the present German society. He had found a true friend in my mother and swore to her that he had never confided this to anyone. He had an attraction to so many men wherever he went. His frustration was absolute. My mother told me that she was not 100% sure that he was telling her the truth. At times she thought he had made up that story to try to get closer to her and not have her notice that when he was doing a gynecological or a physical exam, he was over doing the touching and feeling part. However, she was never able to determine the truth to that matter.

One person she was sure about was her benefactor Hans. He was such a dear and concerned person. She considered him as totally for real. Since they shared the room and the bed. Many a time she accidentally would come out naked to the room in his presence and he would look away, so as to not embarrass her. He kept up the show in front of the other officers and always spoke of her as his wife. One day he told her that the same SS officer that had groped her in the beginning had asked him, as Hans was in reality his commanding officer, about her Jewishness. Hans had immediately responded that, "As soon as we get to Berlin, not only will she convert but we will marry in my church." He indicated that his uncle was a well-known clergyman and that he had already arranged everything, once the war is over. The SS officer then said. "Dear Haupt Commander, she has to convert before she has the child. If the child is born before her conversion he will be born to a Jewish womb which is not acceptable. The Jews will always consider the baby as Jewish, you know how they are." To this Hans answered, "You have a point there, I will remedy the problem. Thank you for your interest and advice."

By now my mother was well-known by everyone in the

camp. She had the undivided attention and respect by the officers and the regular soldiers. She was able to stroll around the camp and constantly visited her bungalow as well as others. She made sure that all the sick were looked at by her friend the doctor. She also made sure whenever she could, she would take food from the kitchen to her bungalow and to some of the others in the different areas of the encampment.

She often wondered if her husband, Mendel, my father, had survived, and if he would find her and rescue her. When Hans had to leave the Camp, which lately was frequent, she either stayed in her bungalow, or hung out with the Doctor. She always feared that the SS officer would attempt to hurt her or her child. She had the feeling that the incident had embarrassed him beyond what he could accept. He had a distinct and undeniable superiority complex and he was not going to permit this Jew from ruining his reputation, even though she was able to conquer the heart of the Camp's commander. He knew that this commander could not be kicked out like he did with the other. This one had strong connections with Hitler's headquarters. He couldn't take a chance with this one. However, my mother was sure that if a chance ever becomes available she would suffer his revenge. She could not take this possibility out of her mind.

My mother's bungalow roommates had mixed feelings. A few considered my mother as a cheap whore, who sold her body to save herself. The majority were grateful to her, as she had saved all of them with what she did. She had supplied them with food and medical care, and with advice and with love. They owed her for these things and more. The only one that knew the reality of the situation was her very close friend Marcella, the mid-wife. My mother had confided in her. She needed to have someone to talk to and trust. One day Marcella asked my mother "Theresa what are you going to do. In around five or six weeks you will have your baby. If it's a boy, you will need to have him circumcised. Haim here has circumcised before he is a Moil, but he doesn't have the instruments and his pulse is not healthy, his hands shake every time he holds something. Theresa answered, look Marcella there is another problem that I have avoided telling you about. Hans is being pressured by that bastard SS officer to convert me to his Christian religion before I have the baby, so that I won't be able to say that my baby was born Jewish, because of my Jewish womb. Hans has asked me to do a make-believe conversion. I do not know the implications. Hans is a Lutheran. There are no Lutheran clergy around here. He might bring one from Germany. He is really trying to protect me. "Oh my God. You really have a problem." The circumcision will not be a problem, I have already spoken to my friend the doctor and he will do it without anyone knowing. I will have Haim give me the Blessing (The Braja) and I will say it." "But Theresa, the Braja has to be said by a man, not a woman." "Marcella, these circumstances are not normal, we can't do everything that an observant Jew does. We are in war and we are prisoners. We are lucky to have survived so far. We don't know what is going to happen to us. The future generations will understand these extraordinary circumstances."

That same week Hans brought a priest from a nearby German installation and he collaborated with them knowing the extreme pressure of the SS officer who the priest also was afraid of. He sat with my mother in a room and thought her all the rules and regulations of the bible and their customs. The Lutherans believe that a person is not saved by being good, but only by God's grace through faith. Lutherans do want to follow God's commandments, not because they are afraid that God will send them to hell, but because they are thankful that God loves them and has given them heaven. After the sessions he welcomed her as a Baptist in front of all the officers including the SS instigating officer, who showed a sardonic smile of satisfaction.

My mother never told anyone but me, of this occurrence. She of course was forced to make the decision to appear Baptist to have her future child be born in safety.

Hans received instructions to report to Berlin and he did not know the motive. My mother Theresa was very concerned that he might not return or that she might be alone when it was time for childbirth. Hans made sure that the Doctor and the officer he left in command would take complete care of her.

A week after Hans left, the temporary commander suddenly became ill and the doctor had to urgently transport him to the nearest German controlled hospital. This sudden situation left Theresa totally unprotected from the SS officer who was next in rank and had taken over the command of the camp outpost. When this occurred, my mother decided to move back to her original bungalow, for safety. At least she would not be alone. The next two weeks were horrible. She was afraid of going back to Hans's quarters and she started having contractions and was afraid that at any moment her waters might break, and she would go into childbirth. At one point the SS officer sent a guard to inquire about her, and she became even more scared of what might happen.

CHAPTER 7

I AM BORN

The contractions began very early in the morning, before that she had been feeling lower back pain and some vaginal discharge. Marcella was there to attempt to help her. Then cramps started, she felt nausea invade her. Marcella looked and saw her cervix dilating. Marcella had experience with helping out in these circumstances, but my mother had no choice, she had no one else. In the background some of the men and women started praying. The contractions were slow at first, then they gained in intensity and then calmed. This was to be my mother's first baby and she was very scared. She started crying uncontrollably. She felt she was alone. Her mother, her father, her sisters, her brother, and most importantly her husband was not with her. She was lucky to be alive and be with these really nice people in such a horrendous place. There was no water or anything sanitary to help her. The contractions started again, this time they were more painful. The guards heard the commotion and opened the door to the bungalow. They went on to inform of what was happening, and a few minutes later the SS officer came into the bungalow. To everyone's surprise he had my mother moved to the doctor's infirmary and permitted Marcella to accompany her. Now, they were in a very clean bed, and with many fresh towels and napkins to use. Marcella found sterile scissors to use if necessary. She also found gauze and needles and special thread for suture if necessary. The SS officer left an additional guard near the door with instructions to wake him up once the baby was born. All of a sudden, my mother felt a sensation of wetness in her birth canal area, Marcella described it as "A gush of clear pale water" coming out of her vagina, they assumed the water bag had broken. The contractions started more forcefully. The pain was constant. My mother felt pressure, she could feel the baby coming out, with the final contractions she felt it move out. The baby's head appeared. Marcella helped hold the head and slowly encouraged my mother to push harder until I was out. I started to cry on my own as my first breaths of air were gulped in and out. Marcella was in tears, she had just helped Theresa give birth to me. Marcella proceeded to clean me up a little and tied the umbilical cord with a dental floss like ribbon she found in the cabinet and proceeded to cut it. My crying eventually stopped. My mother attempted to feed me, I was told. Life continued as usual. The SS officer came in several times to observe my mother's health. My mother mentioned that she was so surprised at his new approach and friendly attitude. All he said was that this is the first and only child ever born in an internment camp. The rules prohibit this from happening, but this exception has to be made.

A few days later Hans and the doctor returned. My mother went back to Hans' quarters. On the seventh, day very early in the morning the doctor in the presence of 10 Jewish men, (a minyan) performed a circumcision on me. One religious man knew the proper prayer by hard and Hans was also present. The SS officer and his aids had been sent on a mission to a nearby city. Hans wanted them out of the way. My mother made my name official, I was to be called David.

CHAPTER 8

MY FATHER'S UNDERGROUND FRIENDS ARE IN TROUBLE

My father became the leader of the now very small resistance group. Marcell, the Frenchman's return, was in doubt and three of the men were under detention. Ronnie had contacted relatives that she could trust in a nearby town. They permitted the group to stay in their barn. The summer had ended, and it was cool enough for them to stay in that open windowed area. She was able to contact a resistance member in that town that met with them and they made a plan to attempt to liberate their three men from the local jail where they were being held. There were several Romanian guards in the jail house. There were no Germans at this moment. The local Romanian government had reached an understanding with their captors. The Romanian guards were very susceptible to bribery or to any deal one could think of. They were hungry and greedy at the same time. My father decided to use Ronnie's services again. She went to visit one of the prisoners. She brought sufficient amount of bread and sausages to make everyone aware that there was food in the air. The fresh bread emitted a distinct inviting aroma, especially for very hungry guards and detainees. She also dressed in a very frivolous and inciting way. The distraction was superb! She invited the four guards for a taste of her basket of food and they all flocked to her. She tried to contain them and told them that they would get some, but she needed to give some to a friend of hers that was in the cells. She convinced them to let out her friend, only to eat with her. The distraction was well-timed. My father came into the building, with his three buddies, rifles in hand, and once Ronnie's supposed friend was let out, they forced the Romanian guards into the jail cell and released their men and ten others who were in because of problems with the Germans. My father and his men changed into Romanian police clothes and borrowed the police car in front of the jail. They left the city without touching the main German headquarters, they were not prepared for such a difficult and major operation. They needed to get a hold of more dynamite and they needed more men. A little bit of intelligence was also needed on what they would need to destroy in this German encampment.

In those days news and communications were very difficult to transmit or receive and could be found only in the hands of a few. Most of the news traveled slowly and was not dependable. The few newspapers were in the hands of the Germans and all the news was fake. The clandestine cable networks were very few and they were one of the main targets of the SS officers. Their friend the Frenchman re-appeared in the scene. He had been able to overpower a convoy of trucks with three new men he met on the way back to Romania. They now had all the dynamite and rifles they would need for a while. He was difficult to recognize because when they first saw him they reacted with fear. They thought they had been caught, his men were dressed as German soldiers. They brought over 20 uniforms they had borrowed from the convoy they had sequestered. When my father asked Marcell how he found them, he said that Ronnie's mother was his wife's aunt. The aunt always seemed to know where Ronnie was. Then my father asked him what he did with the German soldiers. He told him, "I never kill. They are inside some of the convoy trucks. Someone will find them soon, don't worry, I'm not like them who kill without reason and feel no guilt of their satanic ways."

They met to figure out the strategy for the next mission. They didn't know if it was a good idea to wear the German uniforms and follow one of the frequent truck convoys that kept on coming and going into the fort-like installations. They needed to investigate what was the main activity of this fortress. They needed to know what to destroy. They needed to find a map of the place. They couldn't just drive in and follow the convoys. The group noticed that the truck convoys just drove in without individual driver inspection. Could they depend on this or were the gate guards familiar with the trucks or did they have a specific truck count. They had to know more before attempting to drive in with their re-possessed trucks. They also imagined that by now the truck convoy that Marcello had overpowered had been discovered and they knew which trucks was missing. Marcello mentioned that he and his men had opened the truck hood and manipulated the carburetors and made sure that they were unusable, forever. The tires were also slashed to oblivion. My father told Ronnie that she was going to have to be the one to do the recognizance of the fortress. "You are the only one with the talent and the capacity to do this part of the mission." Ronnie nodded in agreement, as usual. She was definitely a doer, a woman with stamina, capacity, and one that was as brave as can be. They decided to take turns and interview the people who live nearby and observe the activity around the fort. They needed to know, who goes in and leaves the installation. "In a few days we will probably know how to proceed," they thought.

This is what the observers reported: "Over 100 military trucks come in and leave through the main entrance. Most are in convoys of 10 to 12 trucks. Local trucks go in every morning with vegetables and other food products. Late at night jeeps continuously come and go, since the jeeps have no rooftop, officers of rank are the usual visible occupants in the back seats. They were able to follow one of the Jeeps and for five nights in a row, the same jeep ended up in a cabaret in the northern part of the city. The neighbors didn't have much to report. They had been intimidated by the constant visits by

SS guards searching for Jews and for underground members. However, Ronnie was able to talk to an older lady who said that from her balcony she could hear dancing music coming from one of the nearby buildings, real late at night. She permitted Ronnie to stay over one night to hear for herself. That night there was no music, but the lady seemed believable.

Ronnie accompanied Marcell to the cabaret dressed to be taken as a Gypsy. The place was full of Germans and many women who worked as waitresses had little or no clothes. They only stayed for a few minutes left because they knew that they would be visible and probably interrogated by a SS guard group who was alerted every time the street door opened, and one of the SS guards would ask for ID. They decided that this was the place that Ronnie would need to get a job. All the Germans seemed to be consuming alcohol and were evidently a bit unruly. The only ones not drinking seemed to be the SS group. They were like the watchdogs. Almost all the other Germans were officers. This was not a place for regular soldiers, was my father's group conclusion.

The next day Ronnie came to the cabaret and asked for a job. She came dressed appropriately for such a position, so the owner immediately hired her and told her his rules for his place. The SS will do a check up on you. They are afraid of spies. So, bring your ID and proof of address, and other documents so they see you are inoffensive and not a danger to their men. She told him that she had lost all her documents, and all she needed was some money and a place to stay. She told him she was from a rural village very far from here. He evidently liked what he saw in Ronnie and sent her with money to a printing shop near the cabaret, to talk to Anton. He wrote a note to Anton with instructions in a sealed envelope. He told her to come back as soon as she had the IDs that he would make for her. He reassured her that she had a job and she could sleep in the second floor of his cabaret with three of the other girls. He told her that, no man was allowed to stay overnight in the second-floor apartment. "I don't want the police to raid me. What you do privately is not my business. My business is that you entertain and make the customers consume as much as possible."

As soon as she left the establishment, Marcello and my father who waited nearby, in case they were needed, continued to walk with her as she explained every detail of the conversation. Marcell took the envelope and tore it open to see the contents. He did not want to take a risk as he didn't know the reliability of the cabaret owner. The letter was plain and simple. "Make an ID for this new girl so that she passes the cabarets SS inspector's test. I think she will be a good bar girl. I will pay you later." They found a place to buy an envelope and put the letter into it. They wanted to take no chances on having unexpected problems. After two hours, Ronnie walked out of the printing shop with a new identity and very original looking documents. The documents were made on old paper, so they did not look new.

This guy was an expert. She had been finger-printed and a photo of her appeared on a travel permit with a one-year expiration date.

That afternoon Ronnie was instructed on how to talk and treat the clients. She was given clothes to wear with a very revealing cut. At exactly eight pm the SS guards came in to eat and the owner introduced Ronnie as a new girl. He gave them her documents and after a few moments they ok'd her. One of the guards grabbed her and asked her to meet him after work, feeling her all over. Later, she told us that she thought it was to see if she had any weapon on her, this was re-affirmed because in the three days that she stayed in the cabaret, he never even talked or insinuated anything to her.

Every night the cabaret was packed, they served very good food and all types of alcoholic beverages. The clients were 100% German. Once in a while, a non- German would come in and leave immediately because the presence of the feared and hated SS guards. There were two cabaret singers. They took turns performing. The Bar girls like Ronnie were expected to dance with the clients. They usually got tipped, but all of them received or were approached with insinuations of sexual encounters after work.

On the third day Ronnie was asked out by a tank commanding officer. She felt he was the right one to obtain information from. She made plans to meet him for lunch at a nearby café the next day. He was a 30-year-old man that said he was single and wanted to marry her and elope with her. He said he wanted to abandon the fort, go AWOL and escape with her to South America, where there was no war. He told her that she was the type of woman he had always dreamed of. He also said he had inherited a fortune from his grandparents and it was safe in a Swiss bank in Zurich. The German showed her the bank booklet, which he said he always carried on him. He said he couldn't take the horror of this inhumane war. He begged her to accompany him immediately. He promised he would marry her in a church and that he would not touch her until they were man and wife. This man was handsome, intelligent, and determined. Ronnie also felt that he was sorry for all the horrible stories he told her he had been forced to participate in. "I was forced to serve them, and I really want to get out." She thought that he had selected her because she seemed stable, was very pretty and he might have found a possible and very probable partner who was in need to get out of war worn Europe.

Ronnie started showing interest in his offer. She then said that she needed to get to know him better and she would need some time to think about what to say to her family if she accepted. He told her that he could eventually help her family get out of Romania. He again mentioned his wealth and then the connections he had in Chile in in South America. His name was Rudolph, and he said that it was of the utmost importance that she keep everything he had said a total secret. He could be shot for treason if he abandons his military outpost. The only thing she promised him was that she would not return to the cabaret and would meet him in a restaurant far from the German Fort that evening. He gave her money to rent a room in a hotel, so she would have somewhere to go. He seemed very down to earth and real to Ronnie. Our group listened to all her story and decided to take a chance and have her meet him again.

That evening, he was there when she arrived. We stayed close to that restaurant. We couldn't trust that Rudolph was that perfect. We had discussed all the questions that she was to ask him and how we could use him in the future for our resistance activities. Could Rudolph be God-sent? Either he was totally bewitched by Ronnie, or he was extreamly regretful of what he or what the Nazis had done to Germany and to Europe. His hate for everyone that respected the swastika symbol was evident from the second he started to tell Ronnie his life story. He said that he wanted to use his inherited fortune to help destroy the Hitler regime. He had ascended to a high position in the Army because his family's wealth and because the Nazis needed the collaboration from his family's factories for the war. Then Ronnie told him a few very credible things about her family and proceeded to ask him about the Fort and its function and its continuous activity. She was very careful about how she talked to him. She even tried to get near him to see if he was real. She held his hand and he started to become very anxious and excited and responded with fear. He evidently had very little or no experience with a woman. She asked him why he had become so nervous and he responded, "I don't know, since the moment I met you I have had like butterflies in my stomach. Your presence drives me crazy." She felt that he was not lying. She then insinuated to him, "Why don't you do something to destroy that fort, you know that what they are doing there will cause all of

Europe to be destroyed." He had told her that they were developing a type of gas bomb that kills everyone who breathes its effect. They came to Romania because it was too dangerous to experiment with it in Germany. They don't care how many Romanians die in this city. "I really don't know much. The SS is super vigilant that no one knows about their real plans and their purpose. They have kidnapped scientist from several countries and are keeping them in a special isolated area, only the SS men have access. I wish I could save these men and destroy all the experiment material. I know where it is," he confided. This was too much. Too incredible to believe. Ronnie asked him what time he had to return to the Fort. He explained that he was one of the top officer brass and had no special mission or timetable. "I go and come when I want." "Can you stay with me tonight?" "No, because I didn't tell my assistant that I would not return. If I don't return, he must inform the SS detail immediately in case I suffered a mishap. However, if I inform him that I decided to stay out, no alert will occur." "Can we meet tomorrow again," she asked. "Can you stay with me tomorrow?" She kissed him lightly on his lips and he melted with emotion. "Yes, of course." They hugged, and he left.

Marcell, my father, and the rest of the group stayed up all night discussing what Ronnie had told them. Marcell decided that this was too big for us and that we needed to consult, and we needed re-enforcement and advisors on how to proceed. We had just hit a gold mine of information.

Marcell told my father that he knew Ronnie well, "I have

known her since she was a child and I think she is falling in love with this Rudolph." My father told him, "I have the same feeling, when she retells all his conversation she portrays the feeling that he is real and so very special. I think I know what you mean Marcell."

There was great difficulty in connecting with other groups in the resistance. The communication was almost impossible. One of their men was dispatched to Bucharest, the capital of Romania. He was the only one in our group that was free to travel and had the proper ID. He was an old looking dressed as a farmer, German road guards never stopped him. He was a very brave priest by profession. Ronnie continued to meet with Rudolph and was totally convinced of his authentic intentions. By now no one in the group had any doubt that both of them were in love. For the next ten days they planned their strategy and waited for the return of their friend, father Augustus. Three days later, he returned with three new men. One was a demolition expert and spoke perfect German.

The plan took shape. Rudolph became our total ally. He made a map of the installations. We had several German uniforms that Marcell had procured. We had the German truck, hidden in an old farmhouse. Rudolph was going to leave the Fort with a jeep and two assistants. He was going to send the assistants on a difficult mission, to obtain an army truck. Then he was going to return to the fort with our demolition expert as his driver. He had told his two assistants to return to the Fort on their own, they were well known by the Fort security guards and would have no problems entering the fort. The demolition man had placed a box full of explosives and everything he needed for the operation under the Jeep. The truck was to make a stop, to pick up his girlfriend and leave her off near her supposed relative near the fort. On that stop, my father, Marcell, and Augustus, the priest, were to slip into the back of the truck dressed as German soldiers. If everything went as planned. Rudolph was going to help the demolition man distribute the explosives in all the chosen studied spots. The day arrived. Everything went smoothly, as planned. By late afternoon they were all inside the Fort. By 10 pm all the explosives were in place. We were lucky that the explosives control mechanism had black cables and the fort's lighting was very poor. Rudolph had told them that he would attempt to distract the SS guards at the entrance to the scientist's quarters, so that we could overtake them. They had planned to use chloroform and hold it against their faces. This should have them fall asleep temporarily. There were only two SS guards on duty and they were in different rooms. These rooms accessed the main doorway to the scientists' quarters. One of the explosives was placed in the front guard house. They had to destroy it to make a clean escape.

The first SS guard was easily overtaken with a head lock by the super strong Marcell. My father was in charge of moving him out of the way. He hid him behind some bushes, where he could not be seen by any passing German. Then Augustus, and Marcell with great difficulty managed to apply chloroform to the second guard, a big fat and strong soldier. Their purpose was to be as humane as possible. However, they knew that many would be killed due to the explosions which were to be set off as soon as the scientists were safe on the truck.

My father and Augustus went into the sleeping quarters and rapidly explained who they were and warned them of the explosions that were going to occur. They did not hesitate one second. They were still dressed in their lab work attire. The truck was almost 40 feet from the exit to the building. My father stayed behind. He was to make sure the SS guards remained asleep. Rudolph gave the order to begin the explosions. The explosions occurred almost simultaneously. A very strong fire resulted, because one of the objectives was the gasoline and ammunition deposits. The front gate building exploded, and the truck sped out of the fort. My father started to run to the waiting Jeep that carried Rudolph driven by Marcell. My father then received a bullet impact on his right foot, the same one that the Doberman had bitten him in, he fell. Rudolph jumped out of the jeep, picked him up and placed him in the back seat. They sped out. Total confusion ensued in the fort. Almost everything seemed to be on fire. The experimental laboratory had been totally destroyed and all the gasoline and ammunition deposits as well.

Their truck did not stop, the idea was to take the scientists to a safe house as far as possible from this city. A group of men were waiting to take them to different destinations in Europe.

Marcell had gone straight to were Ronnie waited, and then to another safe house many miles from the Fort. The

Jeep was later sunk in a river bank. My father was in pain and Rudolph had been able to contain the bleeding. They had been picked up by a farmer who had been ready for this operation. The next day a doctor came by the farm where my father was being cared for and he cleaned the wound and placed some stiches near his ankle. My father's wound took a long time to heal and he had to stay in that farmhouse over two months. He had difficulty in walking for many years after this incident. Initially they didn't know what happened to the fort after their mission. A few weeks later they were told that the soldiers that had survived had been transported somewhere else. The Fort was closed and was off limits to the nearby neighbors.

CHAPTER 9

MY MOTHER'S TROUBLES

The weeks turned into months and Hans kept his promise, my mother felt safe when he was in the detention camp. The problems occurred when he had to leave. Sometimes he went away for a long time. Although she felt protected because everyone knew she was the Commander's woman. When Hans left, the main SS guard, my mother's eternal enemy would follow her, when she went to visit her old bungalow and other bungalows where she went often to try to be of help. He attempted to limit the food and other things she took to give away to the needy prisoners of war. That however was not the main problem. It was the way he looked at her. She described that he looked at her with desire for her. The intensity of his stare sickened my mother. She had mentioned it to Hans, and he had either ignored her remark or said what do you want me to do? I have no authority over him. One day when I complained again, he got angry, and for the first time told me. "Look Theresa, you are the only women who walks around the camp. You are very beautiful, you are desirable to all the 80 German men in this camp. What do you expect? Do you think everyone is as stupid as I am? I have the same desire as any man. I sleep next to you and see your beauty and fight against my feelings and desires and don't touch you." She could not believe what she just heard. She started to cry silently. She had forgotten the nature of all men. Hans stood there waiting for an answer. He had told her of the accident he had, that resulted in the death of his wife. She didn't know what to do, if to pick herself up and go back to the bungalow? Then she thought to herself, if I leave Hans, the SS guard will sure do whatever he wants to me. She thought the only way I can guarantee my son's survival is to remain with Hans. She knew now that things had to be different if she and her son were to survive. She had to really be Hans' woman.

She reacted and answered Hans with a kiss and a hug. She knew that from now on she had to be like an American Hollywood actress and act as if she was an actress making a movie. She had to play a role like in the movies she had seen. This was the only way she was going to keep me and her alive.

One day, a rumor began to circulate that America had joined the war against the Nazis. How the rumor started no one knew. I asked Hans, and his sad eyes were a telltale clue. He then admitted that he was against everything that the Nazis did. He said they were sadist and assassins. He said he was never a Nazi. He had to join the party to continue with his career. Theresa listened to his speech and she wanted to believe him. Right now, she knew that she had to believe him. My mother tried to tell him to lower his voice, because he had started to shout about how much he hated Hitler. She was afraid that the SS guard might be listening in. He was always trying to catch her in a disadvantaged situation. She knew that if Hans was overheard talking about der Furher like that, he and she were as good as dead. She was finally able to calm him down. He had lost his control. That had never happened before. Things were probably really going bad for Germany. The Americans were probably in the war. My mother calculated that it must have been around 11 months since she arrived at the detention camp.

One morning very early, Hans was woken up by his personal assistant. They spoke in a low voice and I sensed that there was urgency in the assistant's voice. Hans dressed quickly and left. Looking through the window of my room, I saw several Jeeps speeding towards the main entrance of the camp. Then I heard commotion, and orders being shouted. An hour later Hans came in deeply upset and agitated. He whispered into my ear and said that a small commando had penetrated the camp and had placed explosives in the warehouse. Our SS guards caught one of them, and we just de-activated the explosives. Theresa told him to have pity on the prisoner.

"Don't let the Nazis kill him."

"Yes, I know but you can intervene, you are still the commanding officer, aren't you?"

"If they suspect me, I can be placed in their hands also." Hans you admitted to me that you hate everything that is going

51

on, that you do not agree with Hitler and that you are sorry you got involved. You must do something. If we survive you will have evidence that you collaborated with the resistance. I will certainly testify. If the Americans have really joined the war, Germany will be defeated. You must know things you don't want me to know. You and all the regime's officers will be tried for all the government's mass assassinations, and horrible imprisonment and also the bombing of many cities in Europe. I am sure many other things are happening which not even you know about." Hans sat down in contemplation and said. "Theresa you are right, I must do something. I can't permit this horror to continue. He left the room and told me to stay there with my son. I will have someone bring food. I will need to get together with the commander of the other camps in the area. I need an ally, someone that can help me."

"Don't leave for long, the man that stays in charge when you leave wants to harm me, of that I am sure"

She did not listen to Hans' advice, and around mid-morning went out for a walk. My mother was extreamely nervous and worried. A thought occurred to her. "That commando might have been my husband Meyers' group trying to rescue me." She wandered with me in a makeshift stroller to an area that she knew was off limits even to the rest of the German guards. She heard someone crying and shouting in Romanian, "Please kill me, I can't take this anymore!" She started to run towards the horrible shouting and was stopped by one of the SS men. She told him that she had to speak to the SS commander. He told her to wait. In less than five minutes he appeared. She told him that she wanted to speak to him alone, and not here. He was apparently overjoyed. He had an expression of total delight, or of the beginning of the accomplishment of his ultimate goal. He told her to meet him in the officers' cafeteria in ten minutes. My mother didn't know what she was going to say to him, all she wanted was for him to stop torturing the dissident they had caught. When my mother Theresa got to the cafeteria, he was already there. She didn't know there was a short cut from where she had met him. He directed her to a small private room adjacent to the room. "So, my dear Rosie, you finally decided to face me. Don't get me wrong. I have wanted to talk to you and look at you from up close like now. I sincerely apologize for that incident last year where I did not behave like a gentleman with you. I have matured, he said. I want to be your friend. Your secret friend. I will not harm you. Please do not be afraid of me. I am not a bad person." He went up to her and took her hand in his. I will do whatever you want, but don't fear me. So, what do you want from me she asked? You are not my women. You belong to Hans. I just want to be near a beautiful woman. I don't hate Jews, so don't worry. He then hugged her, and she almost fainted. He did not do anything else but hug her. He became sentimental and released his grasp on her. He told her that he had not been near a beautiful woman since they sent him to this dump hole. My mother relaxed a little and dared to say. "What is your name?" He said, "My friends call me Erick."

"Erick, you just said that I can ask you anything that I want."

"Yes of course! What do you want?"

"I want you to make sure that man that was captured to-day isn't tortured anymore. Please allow me to see him. You are very powerful she said. "No one in this camp can get you into trouble."

He really liked what she said, and he showed it by saying "I am so proud that you have noticed my power. I will try to please you. However, it must be now before Hans returns. He must not find out that you are now my friend. Theresa, that you don't fear me anymore, can I ask you a question? Does Hans talk to you about me?"

"Yes, he thinks you are a very efficient soldier and has great respect for you."

That did it. My mother had touched his point of sensitivity, he was proud of his reputation.

"Theresa not only are you beautiful, you are very intelligent and you observe and learn fast."

Erick called his assistant and gave him the following instructions; "Take the commander's woman to see the captured rebel immediately. Then bring her back to her quarters." My mother went back to her bungalow and left me with her friend Marcella. She then followed the guard to the prison cell area. He was asleep, they had either beaten him, tortured him, she didn't know what. He was difficult to wake up. The guards woke him up with a few slaps to his face. He looked at my mother, and she spoke to him in Romanian which she hoped the guards would not understand. She told him who she was. He told her that he was part of the resistance. He wanted her to inform his family that he loved them. He told her he knew that he was going to face a firing squad in the morning. She asked him "how do you know that?" He told her that the Romanian interpreter had told him. She told him her name, and gave him an idea where Rajila, her nanny lived in Chernovitz. He asked her, "Why are you telling me all of this?"

"I can't promise you anything. I think I might be able to get you released, or maybe I know someone who will let you escape. I don't know if this will work but be ready. My husband belongs to a resistance group also. I don't know if he is alive. If he is he will communicate with Rajila, his name is Mendel and mine is Theresa. Please let them know that I am alive and that we have a son that has survived. Tell them where I am. I don't even know where I am."

He answered, "you are in Romania in between the border of Serbia and Hungary." The guard came in and told Theresa that her time was up.

On the way to the bungalow Erick intercepted her and asked her to meet him again in the room next to the cafeteria" please be therebefore picking up your son in the bungalow." She understood and knew what he wanted. She was ready to continue being an actress in her life's movie. She met him, and she told him that she would permit him to be with her on one condition. He said, "Whatever you ask I will do."

"How do I know you will do what you say?"

"Because after I permit you to be with me, you will forget your promise." Theresa I am a German officer who gives you my word and I do not lie. Just tell me what you want."

"Ok, I want you to permit the prisoner to escape before Hans comes, of course."

"What? Are you crazy?"

"How bad do you want me?" she asked.

He didn't answer. They continued to the room. My mother told me that he did not have sexual relations with her but insisted on seeing her naked and touching her breasts. Then his assistant knocked on the door. She immediately put on her clothes, and Erick left in a hurry. My mother went to pick me up and stayed with her friends in the bungalow for a while. When she returned to Hans' quarters he had returned. Hans asked her why she had left the room. My mother explained that she was so nervous that she said, "I needed to speak to someone, so I went to my bungalow." He told me that he had just returned, and said, "Your enemy the SS guard just reported that the prisoner had escaped. He is investigating how on earth that occurred. He insinuated that a group of Romanians had climbed the Eastern wall and had overpowered the only guard that was on the detail. The guard had been put to sleep, probably with chloroform which he had heard was the way they operate against us." Hans went on to say, "I decided not to make a fuss about this incident. I told the SS man not to worry, I would not report it. Mistakes can happen. He was very thankful and even hugged me. A very strange attitude from his kind."

Rosa smiled to herself and continued to ask him about his meeting with the other camp commanders. "I better not talk out loud, sometimes I think these walls have ears."

MY FATHER RECUPERATES

My father was the type of person that had to be active, he could not just keep quiet and not do nothing. The son of the farmer he was staying with, suggested that he start writing his memoires. The young man was able to get him a notebook and my father started to write. After several weeks of this new activity he realized that he had an incredible ability to place sensations and feelings into words. His writing was in Romanian and sometimes he began in Yiddish to finish in Romanian. He also dominated German but did not feel comfortable continuing his stories in that language.

My father's foot had healed, but it was still uncomfortable to walk for more than a few minutes without pain. The local doctor had advised that he exercise continuously and that that would help heal the injured tendons. He also started to help with the farm's horses and do whatever help this family needed. Then one day, they received a visit from one of the farmer's nephews. He brought news that the American had landed In the French beaches and had joined the war. This caused my father to rejoice together with everyone. The news was the great hope that everyone in Europe had. The United States was the only one that could stop Hitler. That was the general feeling. They knew that the United states was involved in a never-ending war with Japan and everyone was surprised that they would try to stop Germany at the same time. The farmer knew that he would soon lose my father's help, he saw that he had regained his strength and was full of stamina. Two days after the farmers nephew came, Meyer got a ride to a town close to Chernovitz and he went directly to Rajila's house.

Rajila was very glad to see him. She had still not received any information about Theresa's whereabouts. She had gone everywhere possible to try to find any information, but the German authorities said they had no information. They denied taking or forcing anyone from their homes or jobs in Chernovitz. My father took some of the gold pieces he had given to Rajila to hide for him. He went to one of the few shops still open and purchased new clothes appropriate for a distinguished university professor. My father's objective was to pass as a visiting professor from a Bucharest University. He went to what was left of the public library, and searched for information in the books and journals, so that his intended new identity would feel and look real. He tried to make contact with one of the resistance groups with no initial success. Everything had changed. After a few months Chernovitz was unrecognizable. He went to all the places where he thought he would see people he had a relationship with, but everyone seemed to have moved somewhere else or had been displaced by the Germans. Then on the fifth day he went by a church and decided to go in and ask for father Augustus. The church was empty, after searching in a hallway he found a woman who said she was a volunteer. She said that she knew father Augustus' sister and gave him her address. Mendel was dressed in a distinguished looking suit, and created an image of an important person, in this war-torn city. Mendel arrived at the address and to his incredible surprise he found his friend and war colleague Augustus. He looked tired and much older in such a short time. Augustus was so glad to see him. He started to tell him of the many things that happened after the very important mission they had been together in. He told him that Marcel the Frenchman had been killed in a shootout near Chernovitz. He also told him that he had married Ronnie and Rudolph in the same church where he found Sofia, the church volunteer woman. The priest himself was recuperating from a wound to his abdomen. He opened his shirt to show my father that it was totally bandaged. His sister cooked for them and then he told him, that every Thursday night the new group got together in the church at seven pm.

The next day was Thursday. Augustus managed to accompany Mendel. he was in pain, but my father was an unknown to the new group, he had to introduce him. Father Augustus presence would permit Mendel to join the meeting without any formalities. There were 14 men, no women, present. My father introduced himself and gave a short explanation of his activities. Some of the new men had heard about him. When he mentioned that he was in Marcell's group, almost all the men got up to shake his hand in recognition of his valor. They knew that if Augustus brought someone to the meeting he had to be on their side. The meeting continued, many of the men discussed the recent news that were heard in a shortwave radio transmitted by the BBC radio in England. London had been bombed without mercy. There were many casualties. They had heard of an American general, Eisenhower, who was in charge of the European invasion. Most of the men agreed that it was imperative to block all the roads to Romania so that no more supplies could reach the German troops. They had no external help and knew that they were on their own. They had no leadership, to instruct them on specific targets. Communication was almost non-existent. One of the men got up to talk of a failed attempt to dynamite a far-away refugee outpost near the Croatian, Hungarian border. One of the men had been captured before the explosives were to be activated. He feared Pier dead by now. Pier was his brother- in -law. He asked the priest to prey for him. The priest said that of course he would. They divided themselves into two groups to plan a railroad track explosion near Chernovitz. When my father asked to remain with Augustus group, they told him that Augustus had other functions, and his stomach wound needed further healing. His new group was called Omega and two of the men were from a nearby village were my father had a cousin. When he mentioned his cousins name, another of the men said, "That is my cousin too." They both could not believe what they had just discovered. They were relatives of his wife. This caused a camaraderie to develop between them and a natural trust ensued.

After obtaining difficult to get information about the next schedueled train from Germany, they gathered 50 miles out of the city limits with the intentions of planting explosives in several different sites. They had no idea what the next train would come by. One of the men told them that he had participated in similar missions and knew how to distribute the charges for better effectivity. The other men seemed to be very new to the use of dynamite under train rails. They moved from one site to the other using the darkness of the night to do the digging and camouflaging of the explosion sites. When the first rays of daylight appeared, they dispersed wherever they could. They had no information about German troop presence in the area. My father was always very careful and alert. His experience told him that Doberman dogs usually accompany German patrols. He never forgot the incident with that Doberman when he first started to work for the underground.

CHAPTER 11

A NEW COMMANDER ARRIVES

Hans received the message early on a Sunday. He was to report to a new post in Poland. A new commander would arrive in the next train. This news was terrible for my mother. She started to ask herself many questions. What If Hans asked her to join him? She knew that If she went to Poland with him, my father, would never find her again. If she stayed here, Erick would force her to live with him. She didn't know how the new camp commander would react to a women prisoner who had a child from the outgoing commander would react. My mother was in a difficult situation. Another fact that she knew was that the Germans never permitted children, and definitely never Jewish children to be born and live in a detention camp. While Hans was busy giving final orders to the camp personnel, my mother motioned to Erick to come by the cafeteria. He immediately met her there. He immediately assumed that she was going to leave with Hans. Theresa told him that she was afraid that if she went with him, the fact that she would be identified as a former Jew, will be detrimental to her life and definitely to her son. Erick told her not to worry, that he would care for her. He told my mother that he was not afraid of the new commander, he knew the man that was coming. "Theresa, I won't have a room for you. You will have to live in your old bungalow. I will take care of you. I will make sure you have food for you and your boy."

Hans was disappointed with his new orders. He had gotten used to having a beautiful young woman near him. Theresa was very special to him in many ways. She was very pretty, and he had started caring for her son. At times he felt as if the boy was his. He felt he had a family again.

CHAPTER 12

MY FATHER RECEIVES IMPORTANT INFORMATION

After two successful operations (missions) in two different train rail systems, they returned to Chernovitz. Rajila had news for Mendel. "A man called Pier came by the house this morning looking for you. He left you this note." Meyer opened it up and it was a message from Theresa. I am Pier, Theresa, your wife, helped me escape from her detention camp. It is in the border between Croatia and Hungary. Theresa is well, and you have a son who has also survived. She wants to see you. I will be in Augustus' church tonight." My father thought to himself, "The time has come for me to do something for my family." He read the note to Rajila, she started to cry for joy. Her Theresa was alive, and she had a baby. My father left her house and took an important amount of the gold with him.

He met Pier that evening, some of his new friends were

there also. My father told them that he needed volunteers to help him get his wife and child out of that detention camp. Pier was the first to volunteer. He said, "She saved my life. I owe her." His cousin Samuel also volunteered.

They left that night. My father bought an old car from one of Rajila's neighbors. The trip was going to be hazardous. There were many areas were the Germans patrolled and the traveling had to take place real late at night. It was also difficult to get gasoline. They had some rifles and hand guns. Mendel had gold, so he could easily buy whatever was available in the black market.

It took them four days to get to the detention camp area. Their trip had not been easy, many times they had to avoid being stopped. They took alternate dirt roads going through farm fields. When they got near the target area, they decided to leave the car around three miles from the detention camp. Many things went through his head, my father hoped he would still find my mother and his son alive.

My father still had not digested what Pier had told him, that Theresa was safe and that he had a son. *How was that possible? Of course, he remembered the last night they were together. However how could she carry the baby without the Germans seeing her pregnant belly? How could she keep this a secret from them? How was our baby able to survive? He had heard too many stories of the horror of these camps. Most people hadn't survived. Others were taken to the gas chambers in Poland. Then Pier told him that she was instrumental in his escape. She visited him in jail, a very difficult story to believe.*

Then Pier said that she thought she could maybe get him re-
leased or get someone to let him escape. How is that possible?
A prisoner does not have the ability to do anything. Then my
father thought, unless she was the concubine of someone very
important in the camp. A Nazi for sure. Was this a possibility?
How else? Everyone knew of their policy, to take away the chil-
dren from their mothers and either give them out in adoption or
let them die. How could she have his child in a German detention
camp? Unless the child belonged to one the important Nazis in
the camp? Maybe she was forced into sexual slavery? Theresa is
a very beautiful woman, I knew she was going to have problems.
I told her to leave Europe with her parents and she refused. She
didn't want to leave me alone. At the end I was the one that left
her alone. What happened? She told Pier that I had a son. So,
the baby has to be mine? My God, she must have suffered ter-
ribly. I have to devise a plan to get both of them out safe.

The three men arrived at the very rural area were the
detention camp was located. In fact, they did not see any
roadblocks near the camp. They all carried explosives and
chloroform bottles in their backpacks. Mendel decided to
buy bikes, they were the usual method of transportation in
these farm areas. He knew that it was important to avoid
suspicion. The less suspicious they were the better chance
they had of learning what to do to gain entrance to the camp.
After the third day of continuous observation, they con-
cluded that there were hardly any transports entering or leaving this camp. This was a major problem. They tried to find
out who supplied them with food, bread, vegetables and no

one in the closest towns had an answer. They found one man that had been to the camp several times to repair the bathroom plumbing. He was very scared when we first attempted to speak with him. He was afraid we would involve him, and that meant sure death. He did tell us that every Sunday the town baker delivered bread for the German kitchen in the camp. My father's mother, my grandmother had worked in a bakery in Visnitza almost all her life, and he knew the ins and outs of baking bread. After discussing it with his men he decided to visit the only bakery in the area to offer his services as a baker's assistant. The baker was not interested in hiring anybody. He said that this business was hardly producing money. Due to the war many of his wealthy clients had left the area. The rest bought the cheapest bread possible and not every day. He confided to him that the best clients were the Germans in a detention camp near here. Then my father decided to ask the baker if he would consider taking him in as a partner. Meyer said, "I have some money and the only thing I can do is work in a bakery, if you sell me part of the bakery I will try to sell more and even go to nearby towns and maybe even cross to the Hungarian side to sell." The baker could not believe his ears. "You don't look like the kind of person with money he said." My father answered, "How much do you want for 25% of the business? I am young, I can get up very early and start the ovens. You can then come in later. I am a very active person and I want to be a baker." The baker thought to himself. "I am 65 years old, my two sons left several years ago. I will soon need help. Ok, what is your name?"

My father decided to tell him his true name. He was sure he was going to ask him for documents. "Give me 3000 Leu and 25% is yours. That means that you only get 25% of the monthly profit. Do you understand? Do you drive? Because I need you to buy the wheat flour, the eggs, and other necessary products twice a week. I also deliver bread to several places. If I am going to have a partner you must help me with everything, not only bake bread and the other things that I sometimes bake. Do you know how to make cakes? We use a lot of corn meal in my bakery, have you made corn bread?" My father, Meyer said yes to everything. He asked him if he could pay with gold coins. which was a stupid question. He of course asked the stupid question on purpose. Money devaluation was constant. They reached a deal and Meyer was to start the next morning at five am. My father told him he would bring the gold then.

The three men saw the small delivery truck in front of the bakery and it was perfect for their objective.

They had three days to get ahold of a map of the camps installations. Pier told my father the main reason why they were not successful in their attempt in this installation, was because they did not have a map of the place. They had entered by digging a small tunnel under one of the weakest portion of the fence surrounding the detention camp. He was caught because in the middle of the night he was disoriented, Pier said, he did not know his way to the tunnel. He searched and searched and could not find his recently dug tunnel, after placing the dynamite in several buildings. He did mention that there were at least 90 small housing units. Theresa had re-ferred to them as bungalows. "This is where the prisoners are housed, I think," he said. "Theresa's bungalow was number #76. She insisted that I remember that number and tell you."

We went back to the town plumber's shop and offered him several gold coins with the condition that he draw a map of the camp. "We want you to draw only what you remem-ber," we insisted. What his mother's father had thought him, that money talks, was proven with the plumber. When of-fered the gold, he stopped worrying about getting involved and the possibility of ending up dead.

CHAPTER 13

THE DAY IS NEAR

On the day before Hans was to leave, he became really upset and nasty with my mother. He realized that he was losing her forever and today a terrible, and until this moment, not visible character trait appeared. He attempted to convince her one last time to come with him. When she definitely said, no for the tenth time. He approached her saying Theresa" I didn't want to tell you, but you give me no choice, since you refuse to come with me I have to tell you the truth. I am the real father of your son, the baby is mine."

"What? Don't play around with me. I have suffered enough, she said. You never had sexual intercourse with me because of your accident."

"The story about the accident is true. However, when you finally decided to stay with me. I noticed that I had regained the possibility of an erection. Your closeness to my body, your beauty and your sensual smell, captivated me. I decided to place one of the sleeping pills that I use, in your tea. I had

70

several sexual encounters without you waking up. I cleaned up your area afterwards. I knew you would never forgive me, if you discovered my deceit."

Theresa almost fainted after hearing his terrible confession. She did not believe a word he said. She did not have any sexual experience with a man other than my father. However, she believed that a woman knows when someone has had a sexual act with her, even if she was drugged and asleep. "So, Theresa I have a right to my son." She told me that she cried uncontrollably. He was blackmailing her into leaving with her. She understood that if she did not comply with his request, Hans was going to take her child, me, away from her. After a few minutes she calmed down. She said she needed to see the doctor. She complained of strong pain in her appendix area. He went to get the doctor and what she did was extraordinary. She went out of the room and went straight to Erick's officer quarters and asked him to follow her. He did not understand her request, but he followed her anyway. She asked him to wait outside of Hans' quarters for a few minutes. Hans returned with the doctor. Hans saw Erick outside of his quarters. Theresa asked the doctor to wait outside for a moment, I feel a little better she told him. Then she closed the door with Hans inside and told him. "If you take away my son, I will go out and call Erick and tell him your true opinion of Hitler, your true opinion of the Gestapo. I will tell him everything you have confided in me. I have a good memory and I won't forget one detail. So please decide now. I won't hesitate to destroy you. You are an evil man. You fooled me into be-lieving in you. You are attempting to destroy my life."

Erick knocked on the door. The doctor had explained to Erick, why Hans had called him in. Hans opened the door and invited both men into his quarters. He started by saying that Theresa's pain had subsided, and it was probably due to natural nerves or stress. He explained, because he had to leave and that he could not take her with him. "The place that I was assigned to is a horrible place and a small child would be totally out of place. I want both of you to help take care of Theresa's son, our son. I will return for her as soon as I can. They both will be safer here in our detention camp." They both shook hands with their commander and exited the quarters. Theresa stayed on. Hans then looked at her with hatred and said, "I got what I deserved," and left the room. He must have left very early that afternoon, because, he never came back to say good-by.

The next day Erick had her move to her bungalow with me. There was no other place he could find for her.

They had to prepare the commanders quarters, the new camp commander would arrive soon.

CHAPTER 14

THE BAKERY WAS NOT THE SOLUTION

At exactly five am Mendel showed up at the bakery. The owner was already there. He paid the agreed amount of gold coins and started to help immediately. The baker was very happy that he had achieved a good transaction and had more gold coins to save for the future, when he wouldn't be able to work anymore. This man Mendel gave him a very good impression. He was a hard worker and did know a lot about baking. After working with the baker and meeting the baker's wife Mendel felt very guilty of the consequences that the baker will face when the Germans come after him. He discussed the problem with his men. They decided to explore another alternative. Pier showed them the spot where they had made the tunnel. Samuel, Pier's cousin, the other man with them, decided to see if he could re-enter the camp from the same tunnel they had dug in their first attempt, and see if the tunnel had been sealed. When he came back four hours later, he happily informed us that the tunnel was intact. They had left a small bush covering to hide the opening portion and it remained there without any change. My father decided to tell the baker that he had received a message from his family and had to leave. He was sorry for the rush. I don't think I can return. "You keep the gold" he told him. The man was really correct. He insisted in returning the gold coins to my father.

They now had a hand-sketched map, and they had chosen the day. It was to be Monday night. They needed an escape vehicle. That was going to be a real problem. The group did not want to involve innocent people by taking over someone's car. They had decided that they needed a big vehicle because they were going to be five and had to reach the place where my father had left his old car. That was at least three miles from the camp. They did not know if the escape through the tunnel was possible, with a baby it was going to be very difficult. They decided that they would take over one of the German's trucks or Jeeps. They had to take a chance, they didn't know what they would find. They had an idea where bungalow #76 was. The plumber thought that it was in the eastern part of the camp. He also said that the bungalows had a number in front of the doors. The tunnel was in the northern part of the camp. The camp entrance was also near the tunnel. They had no idea of the distances between the different areas on the map. They planned to place explosives only in the German headquarters and in the main entrance building. If possible, the main gate would be eliminated and some of the prisoners could maybe escape in the tumult that they planned to create.

Mendel went to check out the tunnel. He wanted to see if the heavy rain that was falling would affect their plan. He decided that it definitely was going to be difficult to escape through such a narrow space. There was hardly room for him to crawl into, and he was skinny, he was underweight. The tunnel was surprisingly dry, the rain had not, flooded it, then all of a sudden, he had an impulse to continue crawling until he reached the inside of the camp side. It was seven pm and soon it would be very dark. He decided to wait. His clothes were black. He could not see anyone in the area, maybe because of the rain. His adrenalin surged, and he decided to take a chance and explore. There was no noise, it was so quite that all he could hear was the continuous rain falling. Initially he crawled in different directions to orient himself. Then he approached the building that was right by the entrance guard post. He saw a light and then heard music. He decided to go around the building and then he saw rows of small housing units. He assumed he had reached the so-called bungalows. Since the rain was really heavy he dared to continue. He passed bungalow number #51 and then #53 and then #55. He decided that the even-numbered bungalows were on the opposite side of the open yard. It was too risky for him to go out into the open yard. Then a Jeep entered the camp and continued on to an area within his visual reach. After approaching the side of one of the bungalows, he noticed that it a had sliding latch lock. So, all that was necessary was to unlock the mechanism by simply sliding it, and the door would open. The windows were high and only reachable with a ladder. There were no lights in the bungalows. That was strange, maybe the bungalows had no lighting. Maybe the guards shut them off at a certain hour. It was too early, it wasn't eight o'clock yet. Then all of a sudden, he darted across the yard to the other bungalow site. The nervous reaction prompted him to hide in between bungalows number 56 and 58. He saw no movement anywhere and proceeded slowly but steadily to his objective bungalow #76. He went around the back portion and heard a baby cry. That was his son, me. After a few moments of tachycardia, my father decided that he had risked his life just to be sure that the plan was possible. It was time to return. He walked slowly across the yard, and zig zagged his way between the odd numbered bungalows. He then reached the tunnel, re-placed the weed bush to hide it and practically slid his way back to the outside entrance. He was soaking wet and full of mud. He bicycled his way back to the small inn where they were staying. His friends were so glad to see him return, it was after 10pm. They thought he had been caught.

After analyzing the plumber's map, Mendel was able to detail the target positions with more precision. He mentioned that it would have been great if they had access to German uniforms. His recollection of the past missions, where his former group abandoned a dozen uniforms made him ask Pier, "Have you seen a tailor shop in this town?

The next morning Pier, got up very early and inquired. The inn keeper suggested that they talk to Mrs. Gramcu. "She works from her house and is the only person that he knows that does tailoring." Mendel decided to visit her. As soon as he met her, he knew that she was not the friendly, easy to talk to person. She greeted my father with "What do you want, I'm busy." He assumed that when she saw a young un-shaven, poorly dressed man like him, she didn't see any purpose in dealing with a moneyless individual. Meyer took out one of the small gold coins to show her that he had economic means. She looked up, took the coin to see if it was real. She even bit it to see if it was gold and not a chocolate covered with tin gold foil. Mendel laughed at her distrust, and said, "Don't bite too hard, you might fracture your teeth." That remark, and the gold coin piece, made her change her mood. She stopped sewing and asked him, "What can I do for you," but this time, in an elegant and nice-mannered voice. The change of attitude was astounding.

"I need to buy a jacket and maybe some pants."

"I don't sell clothes, I repair only."

"I'm looking for something that I need right now. Do you have something I can borrow?"

She thought he was crazy.

"I don't have the time to go to the nearest shop, it's 30 miles from here, I am told."

"Let's see, I might have something that was brought to repair and never picked up, give me a few minutes." She left to go up a staircase to the upper part of her house. My father took advantage of the moment to search an open closet that was right in front of him. Bingo! He saw a rack full of German uniforms. She shouted down to him, "Give me a few minutes, I am searching for those clothes." Meyer took the first three German jackets he saw and put them outside of the woman's house in a garbage dumpster. Two minutes later, she returned with a pair of pants and a jacket. "Try these on." The Jacket was perfect, the pants very loose. She said, "Give me an hour and I will fix them for you." He said, "You know what, the Jacket will do. I have a decent pair of pants." She calculated its price and returned some change in Romanian Leu. She put the jacket in a bag, and Meyer left. After Mr. Gramcu closed the door he helped himself to the German uniform jackets from the garbage container. He drove away in his bike in a hurry. He didn't think she would find out of the missing pieces today. The uniforms had not been repaired yet. All the three jackets were too large for them. However, in the darkness of the night no one will be able to notice that detail. Samuel and Pier were astounded at my father's convincing abilities.

CHAPTER 15

AGONY AND DESPAIR

Two days later, was the chosen Monday. The new detention center commander had arrived by midday. The complete German camp brigade were present in their best uniforms to greet and welcome their new boss. Erick handed over the command baton to Commander Hendrik Watzkin, an older army officer. That evening uncommon festivities were planned as part of the protocol. They consisted mainly of better food and beer for all the soldiers, and excellent food and liquor for the officers. My mother had been invited to attend. Erick had spoken to her several times. Last night he wanted to meet with her late at night, the very strong, rain downfall made this request almost impossible. She knew what he wanted from her, and the heavy rain was a good excuse for the postponement. Erick had told her that it was important that she come to the dinner. He had to introduce her to the new commander. He had to explain her presence and the fact that she had a baby in a German detention camp. The special welcome dinner was an ideal moment to break the news with her actual presence. She only had one dress that Hans had brought her from one of his trips. Erick's insistence that she come, and her fear of how the new commander would react to her, had kept her awake all night. Her baby had a bad night also, I kept on crying and woke up everyone in our bungalow, she told me. She warned her friend Marcella that she would have to care for her son that evening and she explained why. Theresa started to get ready at 6:30 pm. At that hour, a guard came to the bungalow to escort her to the officer's quarters. The rain had started again. The guard came prepared with an umbrella, Erick didn't want her to have any excuses not to attend.

CHAPTER 16

THE DAY HAS FINALLY ARRIVED

T he three men were ready. The bad weather was perfect for them, at five pm it started to rain again. The three made their way to the detention camp. They had their explosives and their chloroform bottles, their German uniform jackets also, in their backpacks. Samuel had wrapped the explosives in waterproof bags. They knew if these got wet, everything was ruined. They reached the tunnel area, hid the bicycles in nearby bushes, totally out of sight. My Father, decided to go in first, he was to prepare everything. He tied his backpack to his waist, so he could crawl, and fit in the tunnel. The backpack followed with the attached rope. Once inside the camp, they moved to an area protected from the rain. They unpacked their gear and put on their German jackets. Samuel the strongest in the group was to knock out the gate entrance guard, Pier was to administer the chloroform. Mendel, my father, was to go straight to bunga-low #76 and find his wife and his son, me. After that Samuel and Pier were to deposit the explosive charges in the three main buildings. They had around 15 charges. As soon as they finished, if all went well, we were going to open the latches to as many bungalows as possible, without letting anyone know of what was going on. As soon as Meyer had secured his wife and child he was to search for a vehicle and be sure that it could be started. That was the plan.

My father was almost in front of Bungalow #74 when he saw a woman being escorted by a guard out of bungalow #76. It was raining, and it was too dark for him to distin-guish my mother, Theresa. There was the sound of music in the direction where the woman and the German were going. Mendel had an instinct that that woman was Theresa. He followed them from afar. There was definitely a party in that building. Everything else was empty. Nobody was around. After a few minutes, Mendel saw his two partners move away from the front gate. He waved to them and they recognized that it was him. He went towards them and whispered what he saw. He explained that, "In that building there is a party and I think that Theresa is in there."

"There is no time to waste," said Pier. "We will continue with our plan." They proceeded to place the charges. Meyer decided to look for the vehicle. He found a garage with eight trucks, five jeeps, and a Mercedes Benz officers vehicle. Upon searching he noted that only the Mercedes had the key in the ignition. He thought of checking to see if the tank had gasoline but desisted. If he tried to start the engine it would make too much noise. He noticed that there was a jeep blocking the Mercedes. He hopped on the jeep and was able to push it out of the way. He then went to the building where there was the party. The rain had stopped. He was surprised that there were no guards anywhere. They must be celebrating something. My father knew that the Americans had landed. I don't think they are celebrating a victory of any kind. Meyer looked through the window and saw soldiers drinking beer and in a festive mood. Then he went to the front part of the building and assumed that in this room is where the officers ate. Then he saw my mother getting up from the table. She walked right past him, without looking out the window. A few minutes later she returned. My father waved to her, he wanted her to see him. She glimpsed out of the window and then looked again. She saw my father's familiar face. He put his finger to his mouth, in a sh sh position. She went back to the back of room to return several seconds again, my father motioned her to come out. She was petrified with fear, with emotions, with disbelief. She probably went back to the table were everyone was sitting. Mendel hid behind a canopy area and waited. Theresa exited the building accompanied by an officer. Mendel saw his SS band. He followed discreetly at a distance. The German was taking her to the bungalow. Just before they reached the entrance to #76, he attempted to kiss her, and she didn't permit that to happen. She waved her hand simulating pain in the stomach. He said something and walked away angrily. He passed me, ignoring my presence.

My father was ready to attack him if he became aware of their presence. After the SS soldier went into the party building again, Mendel met his two men near Theresa's bungalow. He instructed them to start opening the doors to all the bungalows, "Then detonate the explosives."

"Theresa is in her bungalow and she already saw me. I have a Mercedes ready for us to escape. They told me that the front gate guard was totally asleep and would not get up until morning. Mendel told them that most of the soldiers seemed to be drinking beer and would be drunk soon."

Mendel opened the door latch and there was his wife and me, his 11-month baby. He gave my mother a quick kiss, every one of Theresa's bungalow friends were up. Theresa had alerted them. "My husband Mendel is here to save us all," is what she had told them. "I simply told them that in a few minutes there would be several explosions and when they occur, run toward the front gate and escape, we left it open and the guard is asleep." Theresa told him that there were several older people that won't be able to join them, they could hardly walk. He understood. Mendel looked at me, his son, and gave me a kiss on my fore head. He almost started to cry of emotion. He then ran toward the garage. When he got there, he saw Samuel opening another bungalow latch. Mendel stopped him and told him to come with him and see if they can start the engine for one of the trucks. He had four more bungalows to open he said. They both met in the garage and they attempted to start the first truck, and nothing happened. Then Pier showed up and said, "You have to touch a hidden start up button and then the engines of these trucks start up. He found the button and attempted to start it and was successful this time. They drove the two vehicles to bungalow #76. Mendel had Theresa with me get into the back seat. She begged him to allow her friend Marcella to come with her. Marcella went into the car also. Samuel arrived with the truck, everyone in bungalow #76 got in. Some with great difficulty, but they got in. They all exited the gate. Pier then went back to ignite the explosive charges. All hell broke loose. The simultaneous explosions thundered. They waited for Pier. He got on the truck without too much hassle and they exited the camp. They decided to leave the truck passengers in the different towns as they proceeded. They had to get rid of the truck. One of the explosions had been placed in the communication center and they were sure that it didn't survive the explosive blasts. The news of the detention camp attack would not reach anyone tonight. Mendel went straight to the place where he had left his car. He ditched the Mercedes in a gully and continued driving toward Constanta. He had found two gasoline reserve tanks in the Mercedes trunk and took them with him. Theresa had a lot to tell him, and Mendel had a lot to tell her. Both agreed there was absolutely no doubt in their minds that God had a hand in their rescue. Samuel and Pier were to find their way back to Chernovitz on their own. Marcella knew some people in a town near their destination and would get off there.

CHAPTER 17

THE JOURNEY TO FREEDOM CONTINUES

I t was early Tuesday, my father could not continue driving safely anymore, he was extremely tired. They had been lucky again and were not stopped at any of the German controlled road blocks. They were with a baby and that was sufficient proof that they were legitimately traveling Romanians. He stopped in a village and found someone who was willing to rent a room to strangers for an incredible high price. They were so tired that this was certainly not an obstacle. They woke up after several hours of sleep because their baby (me) had to be fed and changed. They left early evening after a good meal. It was safer to travel at night. They told me of one incident, just before arriving in Constanta they were detained in a road block managed by Romanian Police. When they asked him to open the trunk of the car. He hesitated and asked the soldier how much it would cost him to avoid the trunk search. My father had one gas tank left and it had German army inscriptions, he also had a German army hand gun. It was stamped "owned by the German Army," how could he explain that to the guard. The guard asked for 500 Lei. My father said that's all I have, so he accepted 200 and waved him through the road block gate.

They arrived in Constanta. My father knew how to move around the city because of his mission there. He went straight to an area close to the port. They found and pre-paid for a small furnished apartment for three months. I can only imagine the conversation my parents had when each one told the other the story of their unusual and very difficult adventures and how they had survived them.

The next few weeks my parents moved around attempting to find someone who they could relate to. The Jewish community seemed to have practically vanished. Many Jews probably hid their Jewish background to survive. They then started to search a way to get out of Romania. There was news that Italy had been liberated by the allies. There was news that the Germans were in retreat. That Berlin had been severely bombed. Then my father met a man that worked for a Greek shipping company. The Greek company had ships come in regularly to the Black Sea port. They were cargo ships and my father found out that for the right price, there was always room for a few passengers. My father was able to reach a deal with him for a room in a ship that was due to arrive in two weeks. The next thing that they needed to get was a birth certificate for me and passports. My father had found traveling papers for my mother in Rajila's house. They had to travel to Chernovitz to get them. He used to know a man that had an ability to print documents that looked better than authentic ones, he would attempt to find him. They went in their car and arrived in Rajila's place. Rajila was enamored with our son. My mother had named me David, after Mendel's deceased father. My grandparents had left several boxes at Rajila's place. They looked over the contents and separated some things to take with them, mostly pictures. My parents found their documents and with them and with some gold coins, were able to precure a legal birth certificate. After that and with some additional money, they were able to obtain instant emission of one passport for the three of us. That's the way things worked in those war years.

We left back to Constanta to be on time for our first trip on a ship, and the trip out of Romania. My father sold the car. They bought some more clothes and off we were. They paid the shipping company after exchanging some of the gold. They didn't know in what port the company would ask us to disembark. The ship was going to stop in Port of Piraeus Greece. Port of Durres in Albania, Then Naples, Italy and then continue to Barcelona Spain.

The day of the sailing finally arrived. There were 10 passenger cabins in total. My father had always had the ability to make friends and soon most the passenger became his friends and told him their stories, problems, and plans. In a short time, the paying group became like a family. The Ship was an old vessel. It had Greek registry and at the time it was said to be one that belonged to the well-known Onassis family, they told me the name several times, but I can't recollect it... The ship's captain and the crew is one thing my parents always talked about. The crew were mostly Greek and did not mingle with most of the passenger except my father. The second night out we had a very bad storm encounter, the ship started to take on water do to the immensity of the waves. My mother and I got very sea sick, they always mentioned that experience, when talking about their first ship voyage. In the first port we stayed only for one day. We did not get off to explore the port because my mother was still ill from the previous night. The second port was in Albania, my father ventured about in the vicinity of the port but soon retuned. He told us there was nothing to see but poverty. When we reached Naples, the shipping company made all of its passengers disembark with their belongings. They announced that they had received instructions to go to an African port to pick up important cargo. Some of the Spain bound passengers complained in vain. We were then escorted in transport buses and sent to an immigrant center in Milano. My father's briefcase disappeared during the trip. We were lucky that my mother had placed our passports in her purse. Most of the gold was in his briefcase. This created a major problem, were left with under US $200. It was going to be difficult to survive. The American Red Cross supplied food and shelter to all immigrants. So here we were together with thousands of people fleeing from what was left of the war.

After investigating if there were any possibilities of

traveling to Palestine, they received negative news. The English who administered the area simply weren't accepting more Jews wanting to settle there. They would turn boat loads of immigrants back. This caused all shipping companies to refuse to go there. My parents started to look for work in an area of Milan were everyone was desperately looking for work to survive. My mother had an idea. Since cigarettes were so expensive and difficult to get. Almost all Europeans used to smoke heavily. She started to collect cigarette butts in all of Milan's main plazas and cafes. People tended to throw out the butts, she would pick them up and collect them in a bag. At night my dad would process the left-over tobacco, he re-rolled the unused tobacco in newspaper paper. While my mother rested he would go out to the same plazas and sell the re-rolled cigarettes. After three months in the cigarette business they accumulated sufficient money to board a ship to Barcelona, Spain. After a few days there, they managed to get on a ship that was to take them to Uruguay, South America. My father had reached a deal with the ship crew master. He was in charge of keeping the boat machine room clean and had to be able to carry heavy packages and given other duties and obligations. They gave them a small cubby-hole cabin where when we were together we fit very uncomfortably. My father worked almost all night, so my mother had to hang out with me in another room. The three of us could not fit in the cabin at the same time. My father slept during the day. The two-week voyage was smooth and direct. Nothing special happened, until we arrived in Montevideo, Uruguay's main port. My parents never found out the reason, but as soon as we arrived we were deported to Asuncion, Paraguay, together with all the other boats passengers. Someone said that the reason was that we had arrived without visas. In Spain we had been told that no visas were required. We were given the option of returning to Spain on the same ship or go to the bus. We all went on the bus. We had no choice. Once in Asuncion, Paraguay's capital we were let out of the bus and period. We didn't know where to go. My parents made friends with a lady who spoke German in a store and she gave her an address where they could stay. We walked many hours until they found the Pension, a type of motel for travelers on a low budget. The owner a Bulgarian that spoke some Romanian and some German offered us a room with food included. When my father told him that he had enough to stay for one week only. My father went out of his way to be helpful and the Bulgarian understood his good his intentions and made a deal with him. "I will move you to a room in the back. Your wife will help my wife in the kitchen and you will help me, repair, paint and clean the 16 rooms that we have here. I will pay you 40 pesos a week plus free food and board." My parents of course accepted and were so grateful to this man. He definitely was a decent man. They made my father work 16-hour days. My mother was in the kitchen almost all day. I was always with her. There was no day off. After seven months in the Pension, a civil war broke out in Paraguay. There were occasional shootings and bombings in the center of the city. People started to migrate to nearby countries. Then by mere chance my father re-encountered his younger brother Carl. It was an incredible moment. My father had knocked on the door of a room that he wanted to clean. The door opened and there was my uncle. They hadn't seen each other in several years. It was a special moment for them. They told each other their stories and their life consequences. Carl had no money either but a family he had met, was going to cross the border to Argentina and they were going to attempt to go also. He convinced my father to go with them. Carl said that "in Argentina there was this president, who has a wife that promised to make all the illegal immigrants, Argentinian citizens." The Bulgarian was not happy at all, in fact he offered to raise my dad's salary to 200 pesos, which was a good salary for civil war-torn Paraguay. That Sunday they boarded a bus to Encarnacion close to the Argentinian border. Once there, a guide told them that the immigration at the borders was indefinitely closed and we had to cross on our own. We crossed the border and continued to walk with a guide that the group of 16 families decided to hire. My parents told me that we walked for five days, we slept out in the bushes. All the families shared whatever food they had taken. They told me of the difficulties they had when they had to cross rivers. Sometimes they had to wait forever for a ferry to come and pick them up. One time a small boat had to go back and forth six times to take us to the other side of the river. They were never sure of the name of the rivers or towns they passed. They only remembered that one Sunday they arrived in Buenos Aires by bus. My uncle had an address of a synagogue, we all went there. They permitted that we stay in a back room and would help us find a place as soon as possible. During the three-day stay, my father discovered that his half-brother Oscar was a cantor in another small synagogue in another part of the city. The two brothers went to look for him and two hours later we all moved to my uncle Oscar's apartment.

CHAPTER 18

OUR LIFE IN BUENOS AIRES

Poverty was the word. Everyone my parents met was extremely poor. No one had sufficient money to buy food and pay for rent. The temporary solution was to do anything that will generate food for the day. Our uncle Oscar had three children and Babby, my father's mother, also stayed with them. We knew we could not stay with uncle Oscar for more than a few days. He had a two-bedroom apartment and only one bathroom. He found a room for my uncle Carl and his family. He also found one for us, ours was an isolated room that we could only be reached by going up a very high and fragile staircase. Only one person could go up at a time. My mother used to carry me up with great difficulty because you had to hold on to the side handles of the stairs to keep stable. She told me that she learned to wrap me in a towel unto her back. The room had a squeaky bed and an ice box. The ice box functioned only when you brought a piece of ice and placed it in the upper ice portion compartment. The room had one bulb only. Electricity was expensive. The bathroom was in the lower floor. It was shared by six similar rooms. Poor people tend not to complain, they were poor, and they remember they were happy that they had a room to sleep in. All they knew, was that now they lived in a country where there was peace and freedom. In this country they could go to a synagogue without fear. The government was stable, and they were told that soon Eva Peron, the first lady would get her husband the President to pass a decree or a law making all immigrants legal. Everyone loved Evita, as she was called. At the end of the school year she distributed toys to all the children of Argentina, I remember receiving one. My father got a job helping my uncle Oscar, set up Chuppah, (a canopy under which a Jewish couple stands during the wedding ceremony). Uncle Oscar became famous as the years passed as a Cantor of prayers in Buenos Aires. Since he could not set up The Chuppah's alone, my father developed a technique to do it without help and in a short time. Sometimes they both went to several different synagogues or party halls to celebrate Jewish weddings on Saturday, Sundays and Thursday nights. My father got paid for helping with that. Then he was very lucky to get a job with a tailor. There he learned how to cut and prepare cloth for sewing. After three months on the job, he got a raise and was hired as a regular employee. The two jobs together made our life easier. He was now able to begin to repay his brother Oscar and to help out his other brother Carl. Soon after they discovered that their sister Ethel had arrived in Buenos Aires. They had lost contact with her many years ago and thought that she had passed away. Her husband had come with some money and was much better off than the rest of us. The years went by and I started to go to school, and my mother started to work also generating some income. They desperately wanted to move to a small normal apartment. However, they never made enough to risk the possibility of going beyond their means. When I was six years old my mother became pregnant. My uncle Carl had gotten a job in the newly opened Israeli embassy. One day he rushed in to my father's day-job store. Shouting "Mendel I have something very important to tell you. This morning they put out a new list of people looking for their relatives at the Embassy. I am in charge of notifying those who inquire. Theresa's parents are looking for her. Tell her to come and see for herself." My mother immediately sent a telegram to the address shown on the Embassy notification board. In one week they received an answer. My grandfather Morris, wanted to send them ship tickets to move to The Dominican Republic, where he was established, and had opened a mirror shop. My parents decided to try their luck there. In Argentina they were barely keeping up with their daily expenses. My mother answered her parents. "I need to wait to have the new baby before traveling." I remember a few things from Argentina, I remember those horrible stairs that we all had to struggle with. I remember that I had to go downstairs to the bathroom, that was either busy or broken and sometimes it was impossible. I remember the white gown like uniform that all students had to wear. They would not permit entry into class unless it was clean and pressed. I can imagine what my mother went through washing and after it was dry pressing it in time for my class. I remember running to catch butterflies with a butterfly net. That was my only toy. I remember my mother running down to catch the milkman when he sounded the familiar sounding bells. She went down with a milk container and had to milk the cow herself. I drank warm milk directly from the cow, there was no homogenized or pasteurized milk in those days. I remember crying when we left Argentina.

CHAPTER 19

OUR TRIP TO THE CARIBBEAN

My brother was born in September and my grandfather sent us the ship tickets for December. My father's family gave us a nice going away party. They bought me a yellow plastic water pistol, which I thought at the time was the greatest toy in the world, I wouldn't go to sleep without the present by my side. The Ship was English, it belonged to the famous Grace line, a really gigantic ship. I remember we had a nice room and our own bathroom. That was luxury, our own bathroom, we could not believe that luxury existed. They fed us great food and as much as we wanted. An incredible change. My parents would let me eat first and once I told them I was full, then they ate to their hearts' content. There was a swimming pool. I didn't have a swimming suit and I didn't know how to swim. At night there was music and entertainment. I watched how my parents danced for the first time. They were very happy. They were going to a rich and prosperous island, or so they thought. The ship stopped in Port of Spain, Trinidad. We got off and stayed a few days with people who I later found out were my mother's cousins. My grandparents had arranged this beforehand. We didn't know we had cousins there. When we got off the ship they were there waving at us. Then we flew to Curacao. My mother also had relatives there, so we stayed there for a week, until we were lucky to get very difficult to obtain reservation for a direct flight to Ciudad Trujillo, Dominican Republic. Willemstad in Curacao was very appealing and picturesque. There were some suggestions from my mother's family for us to remain there, but it was very difficult to get a working visa in this Dutch island.

On a beautiful Sunday we arrived in Santo Domingo de Guzman. That was the real name of the capital of the island country. The government was headed by a strongman who was to stay on for many years and he had the city named after him. The island was shared with Haiti, an even poorer country than this one. We were very excited, I was to meet my maternal grandparents for the first time. They were at the airport with my aunt, Frimale, my mother's youngest daughter. We hugged and kissed and did not stop talking about all that my parents had gone through. We found out that my mother's other siblings were alive. My aunt, Frida, lived in Israel but would soon join them in the island. My Uncle Otto lived in Panama. The war had separated everyone. We couldn't complain, we had survived. Over six million didn't.

We moved into a comfortable two-bedroom apartment close to our grandparents. My father went to work in my grandfather's factory. My mother cared for Simja, my brother until he was six months old. Then she hired help, so she could go to work. Everyone was always busy. By now we all spoke Spanish the local language well, it had also been the language spoken in Argentina. I started school immediately and we all enjoyed the weather in this beautiful island. In Buenos Aires the winters were very cold the summers extreamely hot. Here it was warm all year. The people were generally very friendly. The Dominicans in general went out of the way to make foreigners feel at home. When war refugees started looking for a place to settle after leaving Europe. The Dominican president was one of the only ones to open the doors to the island. In fact, a large number of German Jews ended up in the small city of Sosua, near the City of Puerto Plata. They started several small cured sausage firms and a dairy industry as well. Today the area is a tourist paradise.

Luis Munos Rivera, the school was totally different from the one in Buenos Aires. I learned how to swim and became a very good athlete in several sports. Then my parents transferred me to a well-known American English-speaking school, Carol Morgan School, there I learned English. I think it was a first step for what my family had planned for me. The local food was delicious. I remember the platanos, mangu style, with scrambled eggs that I had almost every morning. The Locrio de pollo. The great soup they made with a mix of all vegetables and chicken, they called it "sancocho" and the

"Moro with guandules," my favorite. I was just a happy kid until I was nine.

My grandfather Morris was a very religious orthodox Jew. He kept the traditional Shabbat and the food in his house was totally Kosher. He did the ritual preparation so that chicken could be, made Kosher by himself. Since there were very few Orthodox Jews in the island, there was no one to butcher cows. That's why the only meat we ate was kosher chicken. Since I was his eldest grandchild, he started to teach me how to read Hebrew. At home our main language was Yiddish. That's what we spoke with our grandparents and parents.

My mother had started to work as a door to door salesman. The products of the moment were nylon stockings and Chinese tablecloths. She walked over eight hours a day, door to door and was very good in this area of sales. She always brought extra money to my father for his eternal philosophy. "Save so you have for the future" Then my mother discovered the Sunday Dominican lottery, called "billetes y quinielas." She would save some of her earnings to buy her favorite lottery ticket numbers. She told me that she used to dream and had a book that interpreted dreams and assigned numbers to the different dreams. She bought those numbers. After many months of attempting the lottery without success my father kept on criticizing her for spending the money uselessly. Their discussions on this topic became an everyday motive of shouting at each other. She persisted in her ways and kept on buying her favorite Sunday lottery numbers. Then one day,

I will never forget that day. She opened the radio, there was no TV in the Dominican Republic in those years. She always listened to the results on the radio. She always put the tickets on the table and checked each one as the announcer gave the winning numbers. She started shouting "Mendel I won" He figured that she was playing around because he had just criticized her again. After the announcer repeated the numbers, she re-confirmed her success with the winning lottery numbers. She then started dancing, and singing, "Meyer you are not going to laugh and shout at me anymore," She had just won the equivalent to over $45,000. This was really incredible! That was a fortune! Not even rich people had that kind of money in those days. The real reason I won't ever forget that day is because that afternoon my father rented a taxi with a chofer who took us to a beach that everyone was talking about in those days, it was near the city, the beach was called "Boca Chica." I had never been to a tropical beach. We all bought swimming suits and went into the warm transparent waters of this magnificent beach. To top it off we went to a restaurant for the first time in my life and ate "pescado frito" fried fish. It was exquisite. My brother was around three years old, and he was overjoyed as well. Life was now going to change for us, that's what they said to me and to everyone they knew. What my father did next was apply for a United States tourist visa, which he immediately obtained after proving that his wife had just won $45,000. He flew to New York alone. There he had a half-sister, aunt Dora. There were also several relatives on my mother's side. In his two-week trip he met a man who was very well known by some of our relatives. This man was a buyer Mr. Elias was his name. Same last name as us but no relation. He bought and sent merchandise to Central America. Elias was a professional merchandise buyer. He was very successful from what my father heard, and my father took a chance and gave him $25,000 to send him the merchandise that he thought would sell in his Island. He told him Mendel, "Don't worry, what I will send you will sell immediately." Mr Elias Singer decided to send double the merchandise that my father had paid for, and told him, "I know you will sell and return the money to me, don't worry." My father took the rest of the money and opened a bank account. Elias was definitely the honest and trustworthy person that my father was dreaming with. He helped our family prosper and leave poverty forever.

When he returned to Ciudad Trujillo, my aunt and uncle and my cousin Fini who had been able to migrate to Israel, had arrived. My parents decided to make them partners in their future company. They called it 'Casa de la Suerte.' Which means House of Good Luck. They were very lucky, and the company prospered. They were able to buy a building for the company and soon after, move to their own apartment.

CHAPTER 20

I CAN'T BELIEVE IT, I'M ORTHODOX

My grandfather, with his best intentions, I am sure, started a campaign with my parents to send me to a religious school in New York. There was no Jewish education in the island and he wanted to maintain our Jewish heritage and customs for generations to come. After a lot of campaigning on his part, my grandfather Morris achieved his objective. At the early age of nine, I was sent to the United states, first to my aunt Dora's house, and then to a religious boarding school in Williamsburg, Brooklyn, NY.

In New York my life again changed, and this time totally. Everything that I was taught was religiously oriented. The school system stressed bible education and interpretation of Jewish law, philosophy, and history as their main educational objectives. The secular studies were secondary, but were required, and were thought by very experienced instructors. I became very religious. This caused me conflicts with my parents and relatives who were not religious at all. I could not visit them and expect to stay over because they did not keep kosher homes at my level. My grandfather referred me to a distant cousin who lived in the Bronx, who saved me, especially on weekends. He was the only real Kosher and Shabbat observant person in my family. I could now leave the Yeshiva on weekends and holidays. That was a big relief for me. The strictness of the religious instructors caused me to want to run away from that school. I wrote many letters to my parents asking for them to consider a change of school. When they realized my reality and the problems that I was having, a close friend recommended a modern religious school in Skokie Illinois, a Chicago suburb. I arrived there with fear and anguish. However, soon after arriving I found myself in a place that I felt comfortable with and got down to study without fear and with new enthusiasm.

This new school had the same objectives as the first one but with moderation in everything. The way they treated the students was totally different. Most of my fellow students grew up in Orthodox homes, for them the religious way was the way. They knew of no other alternative and were happy with it. I slowly integrated into this new religious community and was respected and understood.

I learned of the true values of life. I learned of the incredible wisdom of our Torah and its commentaries. I began to understand the reasons why things are done and how to do them correctly. There were many things that I still needed to understand, and I knew that with time and deeper search all those things would eventually clear up.

Eventually, I had to make up my mind, I was continually asked what my plans were for the future. Since I was very young and still in the Dominican Republic, I always answered that I wanted to be a dentist. When asked why I had chosen that profession, my response was "Every time my mother and father have to go to the dentist, their life changed. They were full of fear. I felt their agony and desperation and wanted to invent something to make the pain and fear go away." This could only be done by me studying dentistry. After I graduated from high school, I continued for one more year in the Yeshiva that had opened a continuing college. Then I transferred to a well-known secular University in Long Island, New York. There was where I continued and finished a pre-dental program four years later.

In retrospect, I have always thought that the orthodox education I received, was good and bad for me. It was good for all that I have mentioned before. It gave me important understanding of the Torah and its teachings. It was bad because it separated me from my family who I hardly ever saw again. I never really enjoyed or got to know my brother and sister when we were young. I missed the warmth and experiences that one has when they live with their family in the very important formative years in one's parent's home.

CHAPTER 21

MY NEW LIFE, MY NEW FRIENDS

From the age of nine, I lived in different school dormitories always full of students and counselors to supervise everything that I did. I lived a very sheltered and supervised life. I had where to eat three times a day, I had where to do my laundry, I had very few worries. Everything was easily resolved in the Yeshiva grounds. I hardly ever left the school. All the sport events were in the school. We never got together with people who were not students at this school, and all the students were male. In other words, due to the very orthodox way of living, we never went to the movies, we never went to a professional baseball or basketball game. We simply didn't know much of what was going on in the rest of the world. Maybe the students that had a home to go to on weekends or on summer vacation experienced all these things with their families. I didn't.

All of a sudden, I moved to a new town, to a University, alone and on my own. There were no dorms in that University at that time. I simply rented a room in a nearby home. I had no privileges. Everything had to be done by me. I had to worry about my food, my clothing, my transportation. I had to do everything myself and had no supervision at all. Believe me the change was total.

I was a kosher food consumer and there was no kosher restaurant or kosher food delivery anywhere near. I was a person that used a skullcap (kipa or yarmulke) all the time. I had to substitute it for a baseball cap. When I first arrived to the University campus and familiarized myself with the environment. I felt like I had come to a different planet. There were men and women talking and interacting with each other. This was so totally different from all my schooling. There were large class rooms, the instructors were women and men. There was no roll call. The cafeteria was full of life, laughter, lines. The food was not kosher. What was I going to eat? I had no one to talk to. I searched for someone with a Kipa on the head. I found no one. I went to the dean of foreign students, I was in the United States with a student visa at that time. I noticed that she had a Jewish sounding name. So, I asked her if she was Jewish. She said she was. I asked her about kosher food, about whether there were other Jewish religious students in this school? She told me that there were many Jewish students, but she doesn't know of a religious one. About kosher food, she didn't know of any place near. She was really friendly and offered to help me in anything I might require, and that was very comforting for me. On the way out of her office a student asked me where I got that NY Yankee hat. I stopped and chatted, and he became my first friend at college. I think I was also the first person he met. He was from Chile. Fred was also Jewish and knew very little about our religion. Fred had just arrived to the United States and was even more disoriented than me. His English wasn't the best and we teamed up to hang out and discover this new world. That day I had my first non-kosher tuna fish sandwich. I had started to liberalize my very religious school upbringings. I figured that if I don't eat soon I would get sick. I also reasoned with myself that tuna fish is a kosher fish and the bread lettuce and tomato were not a not kosher ingredient. However, I knew that I needed to adapt to my new reality. For the next weeks, I ate tuna sandwiches for breakfast, lunch and dinner. I felt safe with that sandwich and its ingredients. My friend Fred, and all the new people I met every day looked at me as if I was an oddball. They must have thought that I came from a different planet. I was also reluctant to talk to girls. That is something that was sort of out of bounds in Yeshiva life. I grew out of that belief and little by little I adopted to many things that were considered normal and habitual in this new environment. My University life brought joy and a newfound freedom as well as obligations which I never had before. I learned to live alone and cultivated many friendships on the way.

On my 18th birthday my parents surprised me by buying me a much-needed car. My first car a Valiant, was fantastic. It brought new adventures and discoveries to my previously isolated life. My studies went well, and I soon developed a routine that worked well for me. I adapted myself to foods whose ingredients were acceptable, although their place of elaboration were not kosher. I lived a vegetarian lifestyle for several years.

My Daily prayers did not suffer because those were performed in the privacy of my rented room. For Shabbat I would go to an aunt's house in Queens. There was an Orthodox synagogue within walking distance, she cooked fish with a taste that I loved. I learned to bowl, play tennis, ping pong. Joined several school clubs. I had a life, after class. I started to meet girls, and even date. It was something totally new to me.

After the first semester, I was a regular American college student. I became accustomed to these different ways of life. I decided to join a pre-dental, pre-medical school fraternity, and was accepted, after a ridiculous hazing week. When I look back at the humiliating and absurd things I did to get in, I am embarrassed. They shaved our head and left a stripe of hair in the middle of my skull, like a Mohawk Indian, on the hair stripe they smeared French Limburger cheese. This cheese is extremely smelly and obnoxious to most people. It was obnoxious to me. They made us make a palate with a piece of wood, which they then used to slap our behinds with. They made us dress like women and go to Greenwich village in Manhattan to attempt to pick up men. We had to swallow a live gold fish. We were given pills to take which caused us to urinate different colors. They blindfolded us and placed us in the back of the trunks of cars and drove us upstate. On this last day of hell-week they gave us chocolate to eat. It turned out to be ex-lax a strong laxative. They took away our id's and our wallets and abandoned us in a country road at two am, after tying us to trees. This was in the month of January a bitter cold time of the year. We then started to get the urge to evacuate, and there was no-where to go. Can you imagine, to top it off, two dogs (Doberman) started to run toward us and we all ran like crazy in the midst of our urgent necessity to evacuate. The fraternity 'brothers' as the members were referred to, had given us 18 hours to return to the fraternity house or be black-balled, in other words those of the pledges who did not return on time were not going to be admitted. We were very dirty and stinky however our ingenuity took over and we were able to find a ride on a farm hay truck. We ended up in Kingston Ny. One of us who was the only one who was presentable had sown two $100 bills into his winter jacket. He was able to rent a room in a motel and go to a nearby Woolworth. He bought fresh under-ware and socks and pants for some of us. We were 14 guys. We took showers, dried up as best we could. We were lucky also that one of our group had a father that worked in a well-known bank that had a branch here in this city. He was able to transfer sufficient money to his son with the mangers help. We caught a Greyhound bus back to NY. We arrived in time to be accepted. I stayed in the Fraternity for a year. I realized that their main objective was to get together with similar so-rority groups and to party. I can't complain, we had a great unforgettable time, while it lasted. Then my fraternity had to dissolve do to financial issues. The group could not afford the rent hike to its house.

CHAPTER 22

I FALL IN LOVE

After starting my fifth semester I felt very accomplished. I was doing well in school and had many friends and acquaintances. Then one magical day just after having a quick lunch I went by the green garden close to my next class building when all of a sudden, I stop to observe this young, beautiful girl laying in the grass taking advantage of that very sunny day for a suntan. Her facial features were special. I had not seen her on campus before. She caused such an impression on me that I went out of class early to see if she was still there. She wasn't. I couldn't take her out of my mind. I started to search for her every day, Then, one day I saw her in the library, I attempted to say hello. She completely ignored me. Then I saw her fill out some paperwork for the library. As soon as she moved on, I went up to the library employee to ask who that girl was, she told me that she must be a new student, "she just registered in the library." She then told me that she was not permitted to give out student information.

I intended to follow her to her classes. She had captured my attention like no other woman in my life and I had not even met her. Then I had an idea to return to the office of the Dean for foreign students. However, she also refused to give out information, but then I approached her secretary, a sweet lady who I had consulted with several times. She understood my plight and hinted at the class that the girl should be in right now. My curiosity increased when I saw that it was an art class. I still had time to register for an elective subject. Upon registering and reading the course requirements I thought the course was going to be within my possibilities. I now knew where she was going to be every Tuesday and Thursday. In class she was going to have to meet me. Every time I saw her, my urge to meet her became greater. I liked the way she walked, the way she moved the way she smiled. I had all the symptoms of what I gathered of a person that was in love. On Thursday I went in to the art class. There she was, I tried to wave to her, because she saw me coming in. She ignored me again. This was becoming frustrating. It turns out the class was a specialized class where the students learned how to draw or paint a model. A young man presented himself on a stool and the instructor gave us instructions on how to start the drawing. I was looking at her when the model took of his robe. She was utterly embarrassed, she started blushing, at first, she looked away. I think she was as surprised as a I, that the model was naked. After the second class, I dropped out of the class. Drawing was not my thing. I continued to search for a way to meet her. I saw her with two girls. I assumed were students also. She used to take the four o'clock school bus to the train station. One day I followed the bus, and I saw her get out and rush to the train station. Two minutes later I saw the NY bound train leave. These moments kept on happening. My friends asked me what was going on, they saw a distinct change in me. I confided to my friend Bob, and he discouraged me from continuing. He insisted that it was stupid of me to go after a stuck-up foreigner. He said, "You don't even know her name and you are going out of your mind." I guess at that point he was right. This was the first time I had these feelings. Bob didn't understand me, he had not had that experience yet.

Since there were many Jewish students, the university had a Hillel chapter that offered a mock Passover Seder the week before Passover. Since the food was free, I attended and so did many of my Jewish friends. Five minutes before the end of the Seder, she walked in with a girlfriend. I waved to her again, and this time she waved back. That took me by surprise. When the meeting was over she exited, and Bob and I followed her. I told her to wait. Her friend answered and told me that she was in a hurry. I told her, that I could give her a ride to wherever she was going. "Look, I have a car I said." Then she spoke her first words to me. "Thank You but I don't know you. I don't talk to strangers." She started to leave, I detected that she had a Spanish accent. I started to speak to her in Spanish. That didn't change things. Since I saw that she wore a Jewish symbol, a Star of David around her neck, I tried again, this time I said it in Yiddish. That did it, she stopped and answered me in perfect Spanish and told me her name. Flower. I said, "Tienes un nombre muy lindo." You have a beautiful name. She then told me that she was in a hurry, she would miss her train. I spoke to her in Yiddish and told her, "Let me take you." Her friend whispered to her in English, "Flower, he is ok, he is a regular student, I have seen him around." She accepted on two conditions." Your friend also has to come in the car." I cannot be alone with you. The second thing is that you need to come in to the house where I live, so that my uncle can see who gave me the ride. This is the first time I accept a ride from someone that I don't know." In the car I found out that she was born in Romania also. Her family migrated to Venezuela. She had family in Curacao, and so did I. She spoke excellent Yiddish. Later I found out that my mother's cousin Haim, was a partner in her uncle's firm. Later on, I told her that Haim had wanted to fix me up in a blind date with her uncle Sol's niece from Venezuela, and I of course wasn't interested in blind dates. So, I missed the opportunity to meet her when she first came to New York.

Flower and I started seeing each other. We went out on dates, always with another couple, initially. She was not available many times. I knew she was going out on dates with several other men. I was definitely in love with her, however I did not feel that she was in the same wavelength as me. I asked her why she continued to go out with other guys. Her silence worried me. Then in early December, when she expressed her feelings for me, we kissed for the first time. Later that week she told me that her uncle was sending her to Peru for a visit. I did not understand the logic. Her parents had recently moved to Curacao, why didn't she go there for the end of year vacation? Her answer was that her uncle, who she had to listen to, insisted.

She left supposedly for 10 days. I wrote her every day. I called her aunt where she lived in Queens, every day to ask her when Flower was expected back. Her hesitation was evident, and I soon gathered that they sent her to Peru because they wanted me out of the picture. I was not good enough for their niece, is something that went through my mind. I received several letters from Flower, in the letters she wasn't very expressive and did not answer the most important question that I asked her. When are you returning? Are you returning? The hesitation drove me crazy. After almost one-month Flower came back she was a few days late for her classes. I had no telephone where I could be reached. I depended on pay phones to call her. I finally saw her on the day she returned to the University. She hugged me and told me she was sorry. She said that somethings were out of her control. I told her that I understood what she meant. We started dating seriously and exclusively. She was not happy at her family's home. I lived alone. I asked her to marry me. She asked me how will we survive economically? I asked her how much she got from her family every month? Her uncle was evidently her benefactor. I told her that my parents sent me a monthly check. We can both live on that. She said her parents and another uncle in Curacao would probably help with an equal amount. Here I was a 19-year old wanting to get married, to my first and only real love. Still in school, no savings at all, totally dependent on my parents. I guess I was really in love.

My paternal grandmother passed away at a very advanced age, and my father was to be in mourning for eleven months. That's the amount of time we mourn for a parent. This event postponed the possibility of us getting married this year. We both would have to postpone the wedding, if we wanted a wedding with music and dancing. When there is mourning a family does not ordinarily celebrate with those two elements. We also had to ask our parents if they approve, and if they will help us until we are economically independent.

CHAPTER 23

A TRIP TO SANTO DOMINGO TURNS INTO A CIVIL WAR

F lower decided to break the news to her parents on the phone. However, she wanted me to go first and talk with my parents.

I thought that the best way was for me to travel to Santo Domingo. It was almost Passover, which this year coincided with Easter. It was perfect timing, there would be no classes for 10 days. I left on a Monday and broke the news that evening. They suspected that I had something special to tell or ask them. I have always been upfront with my things. They knew I was a person that thought out his situation and its consequences before making important decisions. They heard me out. Then they asked me all the questions that I had asked myself. They knew that I had lived alone for so many years. I reminded them that I was nine when they sent me to New York to "become a man." Now that I had found the person that I thought was right for me they knew that I had made up my mind. They loved the idea that her family's background was similar to ours and the fact that she spoke Yiddish was a definite plus. They had confidence in my future. I promised them that I was going to be a Dentist no matter what. They knew that I always kept my promises. We celebrated that night and called Flower to wish her a Mazal Tov! It was to be a surprise to everyone that knew us. My future in-laws also called my parents to wish them the same. We would get engaged in a few months and married in a year.

That evening, in the middle of the night we were woken up by shots and bomb noise. My father got a phone call from a friend to inform him that an army colonel had rebelled against the government and that the island was in the brink of a civil war. The rebels were apparently backed by Cuba. That night was terrible. We had to lie on the floor. There were stray bullets coming from all directions. It seemed like an all-out war. My parent's apartment was in the downtown area, calle El Conde, on the second floor. A few bullets impacted our building and several windows were broken. The electricity and water were cut on our side of the city. My mother had some food, but not enough to last without a working refrigerator and no water. We were six in the house. My parents, my grandmother, my sister and me and our employee. My brother Simja was in New York. We got up to more bomb noise and continuous machine gun fire. By now the government forces had also cut the telephone service to the rebel held part of the city. We were in the rebel part. The

Government portion began about two city blocks from our location. Things were getting very difficult. We couldn't even try to leave the apartment. Peeking through the windows we would see jeeps with rebel soldiers. They were heavily armed. The only way of getting any information was from a neighbor who lived on the other side, in the back of a nearby building. He had a shortwave radio. He didn't know how long before someone realized that presence of the antenna and his capacity to report and get messages from all over the world was discovered. He didn't know how long his batteries would hold out. The next few nights we saw fire in the distance. No one dared go out into the street. After one week of the situation, we had almost no food. We preserved a little water only for drinking. The neighbor heard that an American aircraft carrier had arrived off the coast of Santo Domingo. The radio also informed that all American citizens and residents could be evacuated from El Embajador an Intercontinental Hotel in the government held area. That was like five miles from my parents' apartment. On that same day my father saw a jeep with a man that he knew well. He shouted at him to look up to our apartment balcony. The he recognized that it was my father's apartment. Several years ago, he used to play domino with my father and other Dominican friends. He had the driver stop the vehicle. Shouted to my father "Mendel, voy a subir," I'm coming up he said. My father greeted him upstairs and all he had to offer him was some Dominican rum. He happened to be one of the important men in the rebellion. He explained the situation. My father said he understood, but of course he didn't. This guy had become a communist sympathizer. He had married a Cuban woman. Went to Cuba for a vacation and became a Castro ally. Now he was the second or third in command of the Revolution. After an hour of private conversation, he reached an agreement with my dad to let us leave the apartment with rebel guards protecting us until we reached the Government side, a half a mile away. He also promised to watch over the building that housed the apartment and street floor store. Both belonged to my father and my uncle. My father never told me how much this favor cost him. That night all of us were led across "Parque Independencia" with a white makeshift flag made out of bed sheets to safety. After we crossed into Government side, we were met by friendly military and escorted in a car to The Hotel Embajador. We ate and stayed there that night. Early that morning I was airlifted to the US aircraft carrier by a US marine helicopter. A few hours later I was transported to a US destroyer to San Juan Puerto Rico. My parents, grandmother and sister had to wait their turn two weeks later in the safety of the hotel. I was a US citizen and was on the priority list. They were still US Residents. Once I was on the aircraft carrier to my surprise, I was summoned by the ship captain. He told me that "your future wife Flower had gotten a US senator to send me a cable asking us to find you and bring you and your family to safety." I was impressed at what she did. I couldn't imagine how she succeeded in getting through Washington's bureaucracy.

CHAPTER 24

A RESUME OF THE REST OF MY UNUSUAL WORLD

Flower and I married as planned. I graduated from Hofstra University. We went to Caracas, Venezuela, where I was admitted to a five-year dental school program, at the Universidad Central de Venezuela, Dental School.   The public university systems in Venezuela are free of charge. I graduated in six years. Due to political conflicts, the university was forced to close for a year.   Meanwhile, and during these six years. I worked in different academies and institutes. I thought English to the Venezuelans, and Spanish to the foreigners in the country. To augment our income, Flower and I also did translations for several companies, and whatever odd and ends job that presented themselves. We had our first child while in dental school. Then two others after I started to work in my profession. Our economic situation changed. We were now able to afford many things. We traveled, we enjoyed our children. They married, had their own children. After over 45 years as a dentist I retired. I Was able to sell my practice and move back to the United States. We would have stayed in Venezuela longer, but after the government of Chavez and then Maduro took over the country, the ensuing corruption, total insecurity, instability in all the government-controlled services continued. We could not remain in a country were initially Jews and members of all religions were respected, but with this government this policy changed drastically. We were afraid of going to worship in our synagogues. Crime increased to unsupportable levels. Today, all our children and their children live in the United States.

I know that my father Mendel was my father. I Look so very much like him.

I Retired to South Florida, I searched for something to do. I did not want to hang out without an occupation and searched for something useful and gratifying. I had too many requirements in my search. My wife had made me promise to look for something that kept me home near her and without an obligatory schedule. Her objective was to have time so eventually we could do something which we always wanted to do, travel and visit the world. Accidentally, I found that very gratifying and wonderful thing to do. I became a fiction book writer.

BOOKS PUBLISHED AND TO BE PUBLISHED

The Mind Reader

Body Shapers Dream Team (Unusual People, Unusual Experiment)

The Success of Failure (The Mysterious Billionaire Plan)

The Lottery's magical Effect (The Contest That Changed the World)

Cosimia, The Emergence of an Island Nation

The Unusual History of My World

The Contest for the Most Beautiful Princess in the World (The Biggest and most Beautiful Boat in the World)

El Concurso por la Princesa mas Linda del Mundo (El Barco Mas Lindo y mas Grande del Mundo)

The Dentist

El Lector de Mentes 1 (The Mind Reader)

The Mind Reader 2 (The Invisible Power)

Please visit my web page www.davidsingerauthor.com

Made in the USA
Columbia, SC
10 May 2022